The *Curse* of the
Appropriate Man

The *Curse* of the *Appropriate Man*

LYNN FREED

A HARVEST ORIGINAL

HARCOURT, INC.

ORLANDO   AUSTIN   NEW YORK   SAN DIEGO   TORONTO   LONDON

www.HarcourtBooks.com

"Under the House" previously published in *Bomb* magazine, October 1998.
"Foreign Student" previously published in *Shaking Eve's Tree: Short Stories by Jewish Women*, ed. Sharon Niederman, 1993, Jewish Publication Society.
"The Widow's Daughter" previously published in *Southwest Review*, winter 2002.
"Family of Shadows" previously published in *Mirabella*, July 1994.
"An Error of Desire" previously published in *Michigan Quarterly Review*, spring 2002.
"Liars, Cheats, and Cowards" previously published as "A Good Article" in *Company Magazine*, UK, March 1986.
"The Curse of the Appropriate Man" previously published in *Love's Shadow: The Dark Side of Love*, ed. Amber Sumrall Coverdale, 1993, The Crossing Press, Freedom, CA.
"The Mirror" previously published in *Harper's*, July 1995.
"Twilight" previously published in *Harper's*, May 1999.
"Selina Comes to the City" previously published in *American Short Fiction*, vol. 1, no. 2, April 1991.
"William" previously published in *Zyzzyva*, September 1987.
"Songbird" previously published in *Story*, spring 1996.
"The First Rule of Happiness" previously published in *Tin House*, summer 2002.
"Ma: A Memoir" previously published in the *New Yorker*, September 30, 1996.
"Luck" previously published as "The Lovely Lovely" in the *Atlantic Monthly*, November 1998.

Library of Congress Cataloging-in-Publication Data
Freed, Lynn.
The curse of the appropriate man/Lynn Freed.
p. cm.
"A Harvest original."
ISBN 0-15-602994-4
1. Man-woman relationships—Fiction. 2. Mothers and daughters—Fiction.
3. Masters and servants—Fiction. I. Title.
PR9369.3.F68C87 2004
823'.914—dc22 2004005914

Text set in Fournier
Designed by Cathy Riggs

Printed in the United States of America
First edition 2004
C E G I K J H F D

In memory of A. F.

CONTENTS

ACKNOWLEDGMENTS

For the gift of time, peace, and a place in which to write, I thank the Corporation of Yaddo and The Camargo Foundation. I thank Mr. A. for providing me with the gift of a perfect reader. And I thank Ann Patty for returning me to her fold.

The *Curse* of the
Appropriate Man

Under the House

TWICE A YEAR, THE SHARPENER ARRIVED AT THE top gate, whistled for them to lock up the dogs, and then made his way around the back of the house to the kitchen lawn. Usually, the girl was there first. She squatted like him to see the files and stones laid out in a silent circle, the carving knife taken up, the flash of the blade as he curved his wrist left and right, never missing. And then the gleaming thing laid down on the tray, where she longed to touch it.

If the nanny saw the girl out there, she called her in. The Sharpener was a wild man, she said, he drank cheap brandy and lived under a piece of tin. He could be a Coloured, said her mother, or just dark from working in the sun, and from lawnmower grease, and from not washing properly.

But whenever the girl heard his whistle, she ran out anyway. He never looked up at her. He wasn't the sort of man to notice a child growing year by year, or to care. He seemed to consider only the knives, always choosing the carver first, holding it up to the light, running its edge along the pad of his thumb. When all the knives were sharpened and he walked around to the front verandah, she followed him there. She waited next to his satchel while he opened the little door and climbed down under the house to fetch the lawnmower.

And then one day she asked, "What do you do under the house?"

And he stopped on the top step and turned to look at her with his dirty green eyes. He didn't smile, he never smiled. But he tossed his head for her to follow him, and so she did, down into the cool, dim light.

She knew the place well. It was deep and wide, running the length of the verandah, and high enough to stand up in. Bicycles were kept down there, and the old doll's pram, pushed now behind the garden rakes and hoes and clippers. There were sacks of seed, and bulbs, manure, and cans of oil. Through an opening in the wall, deeper in, were rooms and rooms of raw red earth, with walls and passages between them, like the house above. In the middle was a place no light could reach. She had crawled back there once, and crouched, and listened to rats scraping and darting, footsteps above, the dogs off somewhere. It smelled sour back there, and damp, and wonderful.

The Sharpener stood just out of a beam of light that

came in through one of the vents. He tossed his head at her again and moved deeper into the shadow.

She knew rude things. She had done rude things with cousins and friends. There was a frenzy to them—the giggling and hushing and urging on. But now she stood solemn and still as the Sharpener came to crouch before her. He lifted her skirt and found her bloomers, pulled them down to her knees.

"We can lie down," he said.

But she shook her head, and he stood up again. He unbuttoned his trousers, pulled his thing through the slit and held it out on the palm of his hand. She knew he was offering it to her, asking for something too, his eyes never leaving her face. But she clasped her hands behind her back and looked down at the floor.

He pushed himself closer, pushed his thing up under her skirt, against her stomach, breathing his smell all over her, sweat and liquor and dirt. He turned her around and crouched behind her to push it between her legs. When she lifted her skirt, she saw it sticking through as if it were her own, and she giggled.

There was a man who sat at the bus stop outside school sometimes. He sat there smiling, teeth missing everywhere. Often his trousers were open, and there was a pool of his mess under the bench. The headmistress warned them in prayers about men like that, never to talk to them, never to take lifts from them either. Some had cars without door handles on the inside, she said, you could never get out.

The Sharpener laughed in a whisper behind her. He turned her to face him again, loosened her gym girdle and pulled the whole uniform over her head, the blouse too. Then she stamped off the bloomers herself.

"Big lady," he said. He touched the swelling of her breasts, the hair starting between her legs, ran a finger down the middle of it, under and in.

Once she had seen a boy at the edge of the hockey-field. He was holding his thing while he watched them practise. "Ugh!" she had said with the others. But that boy had become a habit of longing for her, a habit of dreaming, too.

She watched the Sharpener undo his belt and let his trousers fall. She looked at his skinny thing between his skinny legs. "Big lady," he said, pulling her to one of the sacks and bending her over it. "Big lady, big lady," he whispered, fiddling at her with his fingers, stroking, separating, urging himself into her a little at a time so that she gasped, not with pain but with the fear of pain. And then, after the pain, with the beginning, with the surprise of pleasure, a wild and rude sort of pleasure, wilder and ruder than anything, anything. Even the tea tray rattling out onto the verandah couldn't stop it, even the nanny calling her name. He was grunting and heaving over her now. She wanted to tell him they wouldn't come down here, they wouldn't. But he jerked himself free anyway, he clutched and cried against her like a baby, crybaby bunting.

She wanted to cry, too. She wanted him to say "Big lady" again, and go on, but he wouldn't. He got up and went for his trousers, pushed his skinny legs into them and buckled his belt.

The back of her leg was damp and cold. She felt it with her hand, it was slimy with his mess. "Ugh!" she said, wiping it off on the sack.

But he didn't look up. He was over at the lawnmower now, pulling it free. He hawked and spat into the darkness. She wanted to spit, too. She wanted to tell on him, to tell anyone she liked about the dirty stinking Coloured who put his thing into her without asking.

And then she heard the dogs. She could have heard them before if she had listened—the barking and the shouting and the running overhead—but she hadn't. And now there they were, roaring down into the darkness, making straight for him.

"Missie!" he screamed. "Missie!"

She grabbed a rake, thrashed and thrashed at the dogs, although she knew it would do no good. They were crazed by Coloureds, even someone who just seemed Coloured. And they hated the Sharpener most of all. One had him by the calf, the other snarled and jumped and snapped at his shoulder.

Her mother and the cook came out onto the verandah, shouting for the garden boy to bring the hose, the dogs had got out. The Sharpener dropped to his knees, bloodied and torn, covered his head with his arms.

And then the garden boy arrived with the hose, shouting too, pointing it into the darkness until he could see the dogs. But when he saw the girl standing there, he lowered his head and dropped the hose. He ran out into the garden, screaming for the nanny.

The girl was wet when they found her, her clothes soaking on the floor. And the Sharpener had given up screaming. He lay curled around himself, quite still. And so the dogs had given up too. They stood back, panting.

SHE TRIED TO save him without answering all their questions. But she couldn't. They decided he was Coloured after all, and they locked him up for good. They'd have locked him up for good even if he weren't Coloured, her mother said. And the girl didn't argue.

But now, lying in bed with her own man or another, she's always down there again, under the house, with the Sharpener. Over the years, he has only got wilder. Sometimes, he brings a friend and they take turns with her. They drink brandy from a bottle and laugh and make one of the dogs go first. And then the Sharpener pulls the dog away. He has to have her for himself. He cannot wait.

Foreign Student

I WAS ONCE TOLD BY A DISPLACED RUMANIAN, FEL-
low Jew, in a variation on the old adage, that each
country gets the Jews that it deserves. What was I to
make, in the light of this, of my first day in Far Rockaway,
New York, with the family Grossman? I knew already
that all Jews were not the same. But what, I wondered, did
America do to deserve this?

In the end I was probably more of a shock to them. I
at least had had a hint of the world into which I was being
exchanged for a year. I'd seen American movies and listened to records of American Jewish humor. I knew a
ganev from a mensch. But nothing had prepared them for
the goyish Jewish foreign student to whom they were
opening their home and themselves. No one had given
them to understand that I'd feel anything other than right
at home, flesh of their people's flesh, blood of their
people's blood.

It was July 1963. I stood with my luggage on the sidewalk of East Forty-third Street. Even in the subtropics from which I'd come nothing was comparable to this heat. It was tangible, sitting like an incubus on the cement earth, unmoving, no breeze, no natural force to displace air with air. It burned through the soles of my shoes. It melted my hairspray. People skulked along in the shade of buildings. Air conditioners buzzed and dripped. No one stood aimlessly as I did, waiting in the heat, looking up and down the street for the silver Cadillac convertible that finally slipped around the corner.

Goldie Grossman and her daughter Marsha leaped out of the car and pressed cool faces against my wet skin. They held me at arm's length. They filled the street with whoops of pleasure. "Let's go!" they shouted, and I slid into the front seat next to Marsha, looked back as we moved off down the street, cool and comfortable.

"Put the top down, Ma!" Marsha ordered. Down, back it went, exposing us directly to the hot and acrid fumes of New York. It is odd now that, returning to New York, I can smell those smells and experience something akin to nostalgia for the place. At the time I was sure that I was being irretrievably poisoned, and for weeks afterwards tried shallow breathing.

They took me across a bridge, onto a freeway, off a freeway. When I wasn't concentrating on my breathing I looked about me. I saw the streets of Long Island with rising panic. Panic stuck in my throat and made me mute. I nodded and smiled at the information I was receiving—the fashionable exits, the outings planned, etc.—but I could not utter more than three words in a row without swallowing. I cupped my hand over my nose to filter out the heavier pollutants, pretending to be deep in admiration.

Marsha stared at me unconvinced. "Don't ever get a nose job," she said. "Even if you could die for one. Look what they did to me."

I uncovered my nose, startled, and looked at hers. "Had mine done six weeks ago," she said. "They took off too much. Now I have to go back in to have some put on again."

I couldn't have come at a better time.

We turned a corner and drew up beside a drab, grey, two-storey house.

"Here we are!" Marsha shouted.

"Home sweet home," said Goldie.

The house stood on a corner at the end of a long row of equally modest siblings. All were covered in grey or brown asbestos shingle and had coordinated metal awnings, screens, and porches. Some had tricycles in front, or basketball hoops tacked over garage doors. Children climbed over and around parked cars. And over all hung the heavy haze of New York midsummer.

A woman with her head covered in curlers and a scarf waved from the next door porch.

"Hey, Ethel!" Goldie shouted. She tugged at my sleeve. "This is the one! Our foreign student!"

Ethel hung her folded arms and huge breasts over the porch railing. "She's *darling*!" she said. "Welcome!"

INSIDE, THE HOUSE was unlike any I'd ever seen. It was unhouselike, closed in, closed off. I stood in the cool front hall trying to adjust my eyes to the dim light. My voice had faded and dried up. I couldn't bring it back. But Marsha and Goldie took my silence for approval and flew around touching things and talking about them, shepherding me from room to room.

In all the rooms shades were drawn over the windows to keep out the heat. Air conditioners buzzed in those rooms which were in use. In others, such as the living room, doors remained closed throughout summer and winter and temperature controls were used only for guests. They switched on a lamp for me to see by. But before I could see, I smelled the strange odour of synthetic fibers long out of touch with fresh air. Lots of the things in the house seemed beyond touch. All moveable objects were covered in specially fitted clear plastic wrappers—lampshades, sofas, telephone books, table tops. Brocade and gold leafing shone through, pristine and inaccessible. Plastic runners criss-crossed wildly over royal blue carpeting. Glass covered the oil paintings—landscapes and seascapes. Gilded cornucopias camouflaged the light switches.

Strangest of all was the music. Over all the incidental noise of the household—the Grossmans' shouting, the air conditioning, the traffic outside—there was music. The whole house was ingeniously wired up for it, even the toilet. Mantovani was the favorite, but close behind came Ray Conniff, Arthur Fiedler, and some group playing American Jewish folk songs. We slipped smoothly from "Lady of Spain" to "Hava Nagila" and then back to "Pomp and Circumstance." Goldie sang and hummed constantly, occasionally picking out the tunes as accompaniment on an electric organ.

Throughout the house Goldie had surrounded herself with strange wisdom. A "Recipe for Happiness" hung on one kitchen wall. "Smile, you may never see tomorrow," sang the bathroom mirror. All sorts of injunctions in bronze on loving and helping and cooperating mingled on the surfaces of dressers and mantelpieces with bowling trophies and plaques of appreciation.

I watched Goldie with wonder. She was completely different from the women I knew at home. Wearing Bermuda shorts and sneakers and short streaked hair, chewing gum with her mouth open, she seemed wrong in the role of adult. No dignity removed her from Marsha and me. She slopped into a chair and complained loudly about menstruation. She reached for a pair of my shoes and squashed her feet into them. "Nice," she said. "Can I wear them some time?"

After I'd unpacked she led me to what looked like a hidden panel in the wainscoting of the front hall. "Sam's office," she explained. "He's waiting for us."

She rapped quickly on the panel and a door was unlocked from the other side, opening into a large waiting room. On benches around the wall sat ten or twelve obese women, puffing and fanning themselves against the heat.

Goldie saw me staring. "He's a diet doctor," she whispered. "They come to him from miles around. Every borough of the city."

I wondered if the women on the benches were all new patients.

"Come," she said. "Sam's time is money."

"Aha!" Sam Grossman pulled himself out of a black swivel chair. He breathed in deeply, a small fat man trying to be tall and thin. He seemed to be smiling, but his mouth was lost in the shadow of an enormous pink nose that governed his face. Tiny black eyes, too close to each other, watched the way I folded my hands behind me. "Come here, sweetheart," he said. "Let's have a look at you."

"Isn't she *beautiful,* Sam! Just wait'll you hear her *talk*!"

"So talk!" He held out his hands to me. "Don't be embarrassed, sweetheart. Shalom! You understand 'shalom'?"

"Oh yes," I said. "Of course."

"See? Hear that?" Goldie gave me a small shove towards him and he caught me at the elbows.

"Sounds like normal English to me," he said. He squeezed me reassuringly. "You relax, sweetheart, you hear? I say welcome. Welcome to our happy home. Peace. Shalom. I'll see you later."

FROM ABOUT THIS point the panic that had visited me in the car and again in the front hall moved in to stay. It allowed me to talk, smile, unpack, but all the while my head churned with plans for escape. I lay awake at night turning them over and over, inside out. After a few days of this, when letters began to arrive from home, the panic took the form of homesickness, that crippling legacy of familiar sounds and smells and tastes now out of reach. Everything I saw or heard or didn't hear triggered a wild upsurge of nausea and tearfulness. I watched "Tarzan" on the television. I buried myself in *National Geographic*s with sections on Africa full of lions I'd never seen and alien tribes. It didn't matter. I courted familiarity even in the unfamiliar.

And I ate almost nothing. The homesickness had filled up my stomach and I was never hungry. I picked and pushed the pieces around the plate, steeling myself against the family's perplexed whispering and Sam's persistent comments.

"Look, sweetheart," he coaxed. "We could use a few more like you in the clinic, but for the meantime, do Goldie a favor, take a few bites of chicken, hey? Some kasha, no? Well," he'd say at last with a shrug of ethnic resignation, "I guess she just don't like our food."

Marsha stared at the watery ground beef and cabbage on my plate. "What do you eat in Africa?" she asked. "Baboons?"

GOLDIE SEEMED SURE that things would cheer me up. So we went to the family's wholesale houses where they bought me a fake fur coat and hat, dresses and skirts, Bermuda shorts, costume jewelry. I saw myself transformed in wild reds and aquamarines, with sparkles in my hair and a fixed smile on my lips. "You're one of us," Goldie assured me. "Why shouldn't I do for you what I would do for my own daughter?" Her benevolence delighted her. She decided now that I needed the time of my life. "We gonna keep that smile on her face," she said to Sam and Marsha.

So off we went to Coney Island, to their beach cabana, to "Stop the World, I Want to Get Off." Marsha and I drove in Sam's new T-bird to meet her friends at pizza parlors and soda fountains and the local bowling alley three nights a week.

At eighteen I felt aged with these fresh, smooth-skinned, straight-toothed American high school students. My own world of nightclubs and cha-cha-cha and Latin sophistication had left me without the ingenuousness to enjoy folksinging and boys my own age. I longed for someone to talk to, someone who would understand my predicament. And other things too. How ugly everything was to me. The house. The clothes. The voices. The squat bare bowling alley with its echoing din of loudspeakers and bells.

The longer I stayed the dimmer became my dreams of escape. Everyone except me assumed that I was there for a year. I tried often to hint at the possibility of leaving, but no one seemed to notice. I knew that if I confessed my misery to AFS they would set about finding me another family. The thought of another family silenced me. It was I who was the misfit, not the Grossmans. And who could tell where they would move me to? Wyoming? Arkansas? Places I couldn't even pronounce.

I wrote my parents of a mild case of homesickness. They phoned immediately. My father repeated his old boarding school tales of homesickness and cold showers. He cautioned me to stick it out, grin and bear it, pull up my socks, play the game. My mother told me how proud they were of me, how everyone was proud, this one and that one. Mention of this one and that one brought tears to my eyes. I could hardly speak for the weight of the year ahead of me. The bargain I'd struck. Fifty-two weeks. Three hundred and sixty-five days as the guest of strangers.

TWO WEEKS BEFORE school was to begin Sam brought the suitcases down from the attic. Neither Goldie nor

Marsha would tell me what they were for. But Goldie announced that we were off to the wholesale houses again. For evening wear this time, she said. Something *really* dressy. I was mystified. My own evening clothes had hung untouched for months. Apart from the bowling alley and a few hospital bazaars there was no nightlife at all in Far Rockaway.

At dinner that night Sam rapped on the table for our attention. He cleared his throat. Goldie and Marsha winked at each other.

"Here you are," he said, "from a foreign land, and yet no stranger, our daughter for this year."

"*Tell* her, Dad!"

"Grossingers," Goldie whispered.

"Excuse me?"

"*Grossingers!*" she shouted. "Never heard of Grossingers? The Catskills! *Boy* have *you* got a treat coming!"

"What about the *food*, Ma! Tell her about the *food*!"

"The food, the food!" sang Goldie.

"And the *pools*! Indoor and outdoor! The *clothes*!"

THE FOLLOWING FRIDAY morning Goldie took Marsha and me to the beauty salon. We emerged teased, sprayed and stiff, and drove off to the Catskills like paper roses in a pot. Sam was ecstatic. "My three beauties!" he chortled. "Boy oh boy! We're going to have to tie 'em down!" And to me he added, "For you, darling, I'm wishing only the best! A nice American boy to keep you here with us! Nice *Jewish* boy, lots of dough. Can you imagine *that?*" He slapped Goldie's thigh. "A wedding! The whole family flying here from Africa!"

"Hey, hey, Sam! She's gotta meet him first! There's a big demand you know." Goldie eyed me analytically. "How do we know she's gonna like one of our boys?" she asked.

AT GROSSINGERS, BEFORE dinner on that first night, we gathered in a large hall with the other guests to view and be viewed. Marsha wore an aquamarine sequined evening gown held up by shoestring straps and a padded bra. She had matched her eyeshadow exactly to the color of the fabric and wore long false eyelashes which kept unsticking at the edges. "Oh shoot!" she hissed and darted off to the ladies' room.

I stood about, excruciated in my new gold lamé, with shoes and a tiara to match. Goldie, behind us, prodded us forward with words of encouragement. "He's *cute!...He's darling!*" she would say of some smooth-looking character in a dark suit and loafers. And the boy in question would turn in profile, this way, that way, to show the cut of his cloth.

But Marsha and I were ignored. Goldie coached us too closely. The other mothers hung back, seemed to have a more remote code of communication with their children, and never shepherded more than one of a sex at one time.

Ignominiously we shuffled into the dining room and were seated at a large table with several others.

"See what I told you?" Goldie whispered. "Ever seen such clothes in your *life?*" She was right. Chunks of gold and precious stones circled fingers and arms and necks, hung from ears like ripe fruit. Hair, dyed and teased, stood out in horns and wings. Silver and gold fabrics glittered in the light of the chandeliers. There were furs everywhere. Beaded bags. Jeweled spectacles. No one stared at me in my lamé and tiara. No one giggled as I did. I felt absurd. I blushed. I wanted to turn and run.

Sam broke off a piece of challah and then scooted the plate over to me. "Take, take!" he said, spraying crumbs all over his neighbor. "Eat! Eat!"

"Sam!" Goldie whispered urgently. "First we have to be welcomed! And they haven't said the *blessings!*"

But Sam ignored her and addressed the table at large. "This lovely little lady is visiting us all the way from *Africa!*"

People turned to look. Some smiled in disbelief. Even the supercilious young waiter next to our table stared down at me.

"She's our daughter for the year," he went on. "A nice Jewish girl, can you believe? Here darling—" He held up an empty wine glass. "This is to a sweet year. May all your troubles be little ones!"

The crowd at the table murmured and smirked. But before they could ask me questions a loudspeaker crackled on. A voice welcomed us on behalf of the family Grossinger to this their happy home. We were to eat and enjoy, it said. To partake with them of the Sabbath meal. And we should be honored to have in our midst a cantor famous the world over. He had come there to bless the Sabbath wine and to sing at services. Welcome. Peace. Shabat shalom.

"*Now* you'll see what food is!" Goldie whispered. "Just take a look at the menu!"

The people around me were already ordering two and three dishes at a time. They laughed at the sight of the waiters staggering in under heavy trays. And when the platters and bowls and chafing dishes descended all around us, they ate without even a smile of embarrassment. They complimented each other on the spans of side dishes. Leaned over with forks poised to taste, nodded and rolled their eyes in approval. And then, when the last dessert dish had been removed, they wiped their mouths extravagantly and trooped off to the hotel's synagogue to hear the famous cantor.

An organ played softly as we walked in. No one talked. At eight o'clock exactly the rabbi and the cantor, like two plump brides in white satin robes, walked down the aisle and climbed up to the podium in front.

I listened carefully to the cantor's singing for hints and snatches of familiar tunes. But the organ played and a choir sang and the melodies themselves sounded more like my old Anglican school hymns than the meandering Eastern prayers I knew from shul at home. There was none of the chaos of our own services—women waving and talking in the balconies, men swaying and chanting and beating their breasts below. This service was orderly. It didn't seem Jewish at all. The rabbi stood up. He clasped the podium and raised his eyes above our heads. Addressing God in English, he begged for wisdom and gave elaborate praise. The congregation raised their books and begged and praised in turn. He spoke of Jews the world over. They gave thanks for the land of Israel. He spoke of suffering. They catalogued their blessings. The whole service began to sound like a literate version of one of Sam's dinnertime homilies.

Marsha nudged me. "Why aren't you reading?" she whispered. "It's disrespectful!"

"SHABBAT SHALOM, SWEETHEART!" Sam shouted as we turned to leave. He kissed me on the lips. He kissed Goldie and Marsha on the lips too. He threw an arm around my waist and another around Marsha's. "Wasn't that just *beautiful*, girls?" he asked.

"Beautiful! Beautiful!" Goldie chanted.

And then suddenly my head cleared. Just like that. Standing there amongst these strangers, these alien Jews, with Sam's wet kiss still on my lips, I knew what I had to do. The cantor's voice and the rabbi's words that had filled them with such comfortable reverence for their Jewishness, the strange sounds of the organ, the chorus of voices, had worked a miracle for me. I saw that hints would not do. Nothing but the truth would do. I would simply have to sacrifice my parents' pride in me, and their standing with this one and that one. I would confess the whole of my misery. I would beg them to let me come home.

Early the next morning I wrote the letter. I spared them nothing, not even Sam's patients or Goldie's period pains. I ran out to the mailbox and thrust the envelope down its throat as far as it would go. Then I skipped out in the crisp morning air. I stood at a distance and looked at the hotel. Saw for the first time how beautiful it was. A real building made of stone, open on all sides, with paths and trees around it. The air smelled of lawn clippings and freshly turned soil. The sky was blue and clear. Trees grew all over the hills. For the first time since leaving home I felt back on earth. I was even hungry.

BACK IN FAR ROCKAWAY my secret became heavier as the week progressed. It burdened my dreams so that I awoke with a fright. I didn't hear what people said to me. The family teased me about being in love. Who was it? they wanted to know. One of the boys from Grossingers?

By Friday afternoon I had almost grown used to the

wait. When I returned from the library I found Goldie sitting in the kitchen, mute. I noticed that she had missed her appointment at the beauty salon. Her hair stuck in strands to her face as if she had a fever. The polish on her nails was chipped and dull. "Are you all right, Goldie?" I asked.

"Am I all right?" she asked, addressing the air above my head.

It had happened. I could barely breathe.

Goldie shook her head from side to side and then slowly and apparently painfully pushed herself up, wiped her hands on her apron. With her head held high she began to leave the room. "Wait here if you please," she said. "I'm going to get my husband who has patients, emergencies, but never mind that. He asked that I should call him when you came home."

I sat there, mute in my turn, my heart clattering so loudly against my ribs and in my throat that it drowned out all the thoughts and phrases I had prepared for the occasion.

Goldie and Sam appeared together at the kitchen door. They stood still and looked at me in silence, like some latter-day American Jewish Gothic. They moved slowly to the table to sit. Goldie opened her mouth to speak but Sam laid a hand over hers.

"It has come to our notice," he said at last, "that you wish to leave this home and move out."

Goldie shook her head sadly. I opened my mouth to speak but Sam held up his hand and closed his eyes.

"Today I received a call from an important person—
a Mr. Bollito. Bolati. Who knows? The head of FAS."

"AFS," I said.

"Yes, thank you for that. Well, this Belliti he says to
me that you are unsuitable to our home. They made a
mistake, he says, and now they will take you away. 'Mistake?' I says. 'What mistake? *You*, Mr. Beltini, *you* are the
person making the mistake.'" He looked at Goldie and
shook his head. "A nudnik from Yonkers I sounded like.
'She's our baby, our girl,' I told him. Then he says
to me—" Sam's grasp tightened on Goldie's hand—
"He says, 'the girl is not happy. Unhappy,' he says. 'Miserable. She writes letters to her parents about it and they
phone all the way from Africa.' They phone to ask *him* to
help—not me, mind you, they don't phone me, a *medical
doctor*. They phone *him*, Mr. Head Goy, Brentano, whatever. Well," he said to me at last, "if you must go, you
must go. That's all. And tomorrow. Already. The sooner
the better—*his* words, not mine. Goldie here, I worry
about her for your information. Like a mother to you
she's been. And our Marsha, that wonderful child. Who
knows? You've been more than a sister to that girl who
has no other. Did you think of that when you wrote those
letters? Huh?"

There were no words to deal with this. I shrugged
slightly under their glare. "Marsha is very resilient," I
muttered.

"What is this?" Sam asked Goldie. "Is this the girl

we've loved as our own? Wished for only the best?
Opened our heart?"

Goldie nodded. A few tears squeezed out and rolled
unchecked down her cheek. Sam looked at me and then
led my eye with his to the sight of Goldie's silent weeping. He watched me watching and then turned to leave.
"It takes a heart of stone," he said.

The phone rang out. Sam answered it. He closed his
eyes and held the receiver out to me. "Long distance," he
said.

"Hello?"

"*Darling!* Is that *you?*" My mother's voice boomed
through the muffled beeps and crackles.

"Yes."

"How are you, my darling? Are you all right? That's
the *first* thing we want to know!"

"Fine, fine." I stared at the telephone dial in a hopeless attempt to forget that Sam and Goldie were standing
in the doorway listening.

"Darling! We received your letter today and we're
most upset! We phoned Bolito *immediately* and told him
to *get* you out of there pronto!"

"I know," I said.

"*What?*"

"I said I know!"

"Has he *fixed* things, darling? You mustn't stay in that
awful place a minute longer than necessary! When will
you leave?"

"Tomorrow."

"When? What?"

"TOMORROW!"

"Chopsticks!" My father's voice, modulated for the distance and interference, rang much clearer. "You're a chump not to have told us all this before. Why did you wait so long?"

"I can't talk," I said.

Goldie sniffed loudly.

"We would have fixed things before, you know," he went on. "Capital chap, this Bellati. Sounds quite competent. What your mother and I *cannot* work out is why he put you there in the first place."

"You asked for me to be put in a Jewish home," I said. By now I was oblivious to the Grossmans.

"But dash it all, they can't *all* be like that over there," he said.

"Dad! Don't worry about me. I'm fine."

"*She's* fine!" Goldie said.

"We've fixed things with Bolito, darling," my mother shouted. "I'm *very* anxious for you not to do *anything* that you'll regret for the rest of your life."

My heart leaped. "What do you mean?"

"Bolito's arranged everything, darling. He asked us to leave it to him to explain."

"*What?*"

"Call us from New York," she said. "Reverse the charges."

"Explain *what?*"

"Bye, darling!"

Click.

THEY WERE ALREADY standing behind their chairs when I came into the dining room—Sam, the patriarch, with his women on either side of him. I stood in the doorway—turncoat, renegade, damned ingrate.

Sam grasped the back of his chair. "This is the Sabbath," he said. "A holy day for Jews all over this land and this earth of ours. Tonight we gather together to join in the Sabbath meal with one who will leave us soon, namely tomorrow, to go from us and our home. May peace be with her on her chosen path." He looked at me and then at Goldie and Marsha. "None of us, God forbid, should blame her. She is young. She has a life. We hope that one day she will think of us and this home she had, and she will not be miserable. We wish her shalom." With that he blessed the wine and we sat down.

"Beautiful! Beautiful, Sam!" Goldie said. "I wish we had the tape recorder."

"Who can think of tape recorders at a time like this?" asked Sam, slowly tucking his napkin into his collar. He said the blessing over the bread.

We ate our soup in silence. And then the chicken. Every now and then Sam would lean over and lay a hand on Goldie's arm, shake her reassuringly. Marsha, whenever she could catch my eye, narrowed her own in accusation.

But I was concentrating entirely on making myself as still and silent as possible. I took great care with my knife and fork lest some unexpected clatter draw more attention in my direction. I wanted nothing to point up further the extent of my ingratitude. So engrossed was I in this game of self-control that we seemed to arrive at dessert with relative speed. After dinner I rose and asked to be excused.

"Why ask?" said Sam. "You're free to come and go."

"I'm very sorry," I said. "Thank you. Thank you for everything."

The fact that I was not weeping, however, did not escape Goldie's attention. She wiped her hand across her eyes. Sam patted her arm and then looked up at me.

"Sleep well on your last night in this home," he said.

EARLY THE NEXT DAY Sam hauled my luggage into the Cadillac. Ethel watched in her bathrobe and curlers from an upstairs window. She banged on the window and waved. Children on the street stood back as we pulled away from the house. Goldie drove in silence, her lips pursed into an expression of hurt dignity. But Marsha chatted loudly all the way in. She laughed gaily, threw her hands in the air, as if we were driving to a celebration.

When we arrived outside the AFS building, Goldie walked stiffly around to the trunk and held it open for me while I unloaded the luggage onto the sidewalk. Marsha watched me from the car. "Five weeks!" she said. "Can you believe it's been five weeks?"

Goldie slammed the trunk shut. "We wish you luck," she said, "Sam and Marsha and me. Shalom to you and yours."

Then she climbed in and they sped off down Forty-third Street and out of sight.

A DOOR OPENED and the AFS receptionist called me in. "Go straight upstairs to Mr. Bolito's office," she said. "Leave your bags here. Your new family is waiting."

"New family?"

"They've been waiting half an hour. Up you go."

I took the elevator up to the second floor and stepped into Mr. Bolito's office.

"So this is the young lady we've heard so much about!" said a ruddy-faced man of about fifty in a Brooks Brothers suit and brown penny loafers. "I'm Greg Lawson, your new dad. And this is Mrs. Lawson—Nan. And here," he said, gesturing to a girl of about my age, "is Dede."

Dede bounced up and kissed me coyly on the cheek. "This is *sooo* neat!" she said. "We've been waiting *sooo* long for a foreign student! And now it's like a fairytale come true." She flashed a smile at Mr. Bolito.

Mr. Bolito eased himself out of his chair and came up

to put his arm around me. "And you'll find Darien very different from Far Rockaway."

Everyone laughed.

"Where's Darien?" I asked.

"Connecticut," he said. "You're a very lucky girl, you know."

"Yes," I said, observing with by now familiar alarm the pink bow in Mrs. Lawson's hair, her baby print Peter Pan blouse and coordinated wraparound skirt.

"Well, come, Precious, let's go," she said in a high girlish voice. "If we're lucky we'll still make the brunch at the club. Oh!" She held one perfectly manicured but un-polished hand to her mouth. "I *almost* forgot! Are there any foods you don't eat, Precious? I mean are you—what do they call it now?" she asked, turning to the others.

"'Kosher' I think," said Mr. Lawson.

"Yes, *kosher*! You know—" She giggled. "We always thought we'd get a Scandinavian or a German, being such fanatics for the slopes. But we're *dee-lighted* to have *you*!" She slipped an arm through mine. "It's *fascinating* to think of all the different customs and food habits the world over, isn't it? It's just that, being that we're Episco-palian and all, we eat *everything!*" She giggled again and patted one buttock. "No good for the derriere you know!" She squeezed my arm. "So we were just wondering, Pre-cious, whether you would be—what was that word again?"

"Kosher."

"Yes, kosher."

"I'm not kosher." Suddenly I felt nauseous.

"Well, I'm *starved,* let's go!" said Dede. She led the procession out to the street where Greg Lawson loaded my luggage into the Mercedes, and we all climbed in, waved to Mr. Bolito and cruised down Forty-third Street.

The Widow's Daughter

THE WIDOW RAISED HER VOICE AND SAID IT again. "I don't buy husbands for my daughter."

"You might consider his education," said Minnie Kessel, a widow herself. "You might consider the gain for your Irma."

"Consider my behind," Flora Gershin muttered. She was plainer than ever in her mourning dress, with her thin hair pulled back into a bun. She had always had a plain woman's pride, a plain woman's bitterness. It had seen her through her husband's drinking, people said, his women, his long, slow dying. Day after day, she had pulled down the bedclothes to swab at his sores. When he screamed with the pain, she would raise her voice and shout for anyone to hear, *"You listen to me now!"*

Minnie Kessel rose like a large-beaked bird and left the house before Flora Gershin could change her mind. When she reached the bottom of the steps, she stopped for a moment and looked up. Irma was there at the front window, staring, her mouth hanging open like a dog's.

The girl was a beauty. With her dark skin and her black eyes, her gleaming long black hair, she was a beauty out of nowhere, people said. Two months before, Minnie Kessel's son had found her in her father's shop. He had gone in to buy tobacco, and there she was behind the counter, as sleek as a swan in her high-necked blouse. Albert Kessel stared. She held her spine so straight that only her hips seemed alive as she moved from the bins to the scale.

"Your father is sick?" he said at last. "I heard the news."

Albert was a slight, pale, sober man with a sharp fox face and a shock of wiry black hair. Irma knew what had happened to him, everyone knew. He had been jilted by his mother's cousin's daughter. The girl had run off with a widower—rich and jolly, they said. And, oh, Irma loved the thought of that other girl's life.

"Usually," she said, "I help my mother at home."

"Down near the race course?"

She nodded.

THE FOLLOWING SUNDAY afternoon, Irma sat at the window, watching Albert walk down the hill from the tram stop. All week she had known he would come, and now here he was, looking ridiculously jilted in his black hat and black suit, with a bunch of flowers in a funnel of newspaper. She saw him hesitate outside the house and then look up, as if he, too, knew she would be there.

But then, just as he rang the bell, her father had cried out, and her mother had yelled, *"Be still, you devil!"*

Irma ran for the door and pulled it open. *"Wait!"* she said. She held the door wide, and then closed and locked it behind him. "Come," she said, leading him past the front room and down a long passage to the kitchen. "Tea? Sit. Sit there."

He watched as she reached for the glasses, the sugar cubes, as she laid out the plates and spoons, and then bent to slice a lemon. Even when the bell shrieked and the servant girl slouched in from the back porch, he didn't take his eyes off Irma. He watched like a thief, in silence, the flowers forgotten on the chair next to him.

"There's a summerhouse out there," she said, pointing into the unkempt garden. "Next Sunday, I'll show it to you if you like."

BUT THE FOLLOWING Sunday, her father was dead and the house was laid out for mourning. The men took up their places in the front room. The women sat in silence behind them, glistening with sweat in the summer heat. The whole place smelled of sweat and old perfume, honeycake, liquor, and men.

Irma's father had smelled like this. When he had come

home from his women—cheap, Coloured women, her mother said, he found them in bars down at the docks— sometimes, when he came home smelling like this, he would climb the stairs and come into her room, lie down next to her, as if he'd forgotten where he belonged. And then, stirring out of sleep, she would find his rough hands on her, his rough voice rasping, "My beauty, my own beautiful girl."

Irma examined her suitor—his yarmulke perched like a skiff on top of the wiry hair, the halo of dark fuzz around the edge of each ear. When prayers were over and he turned at last to find her, the women followed his glance. They saw him redden when she smiled, saw her twist herself around for him, pretending to look for her mother. From the frying pan into the fire, they would say to each other the next day. What do you think about your son's choice this time? they would ask Minnie Kessel when they saw her.

"Irma," said her mother, "pass the cake here please."

Ever since Irma had been a girl, her mother had sent her out among men with trays and drinks, or to play the piano, or to sing. Irma shone and burned among men, she left them burning and shivering themselves. It was as if mother and daughter had it arranged between them, people said, cause and effect. And yet, until now, Irma had scorned the men who had followed her lead. So why this one? Why Albert Kessel?

The women watched her stop before him with the plate of cake, and then take a piece herself, curling her lips back to nibble at the edge of it. Albert Kessel was almost a dentist. He would understand the beauty of such a mouth. With a mother like Minnie, he would understand pride too, and a hard, cold heart.

But Irma Gershin? What did she want with him? To ride his shame like a pony? To turn it, somehow, into a blessing for her own future?

Irma carried the plate around the room, knowing that Albert was watching her. When the plate was empty, she took it through to the kitchen. "Irma," the women said, looking up from the dried fruit, "you shouldn't be doing this. You should be sitting in there with your mother."

Irma shrugged. How many years had her mother been waiting to sit where she was now sitting? *"Die!"* she would scream at him. *"Die now!"* If Irma had ever told her more than she already knew, she would have taken a knife to his throat, cutting short his long dying agony. But all these years, Irma had hardly known what she knew herself. Waking in the morning to the sun beating through her curtains, she would rise, layer upon layer, as if through the thick darkness of a dream. Even now, those nights were coiled within her like a rope, solid and dependable. She carried them without knowledge, without the desire for knowledge either.

Albert Kessel had followed her to the kitchen. He was

standing in the doorway. When Irma went out into the garden, he followed her there too. She walked ahead of him through the fading light like a tall, dark shadow. The garden was shaped into a wedge, the path curving through it, giving an illusion of depth. In fact, the summerhouse to which she was leading him was less than fifty feet from the kitchen door. And yet, closed in by the unruly vegetation, they could have been on a boat, miles and miles from land.

"A big funeral," he said at last. They were sitting side by side on the stone bench like old-fashioned lovers.

She stared through the gloom at his hands, folded on one knee. She had noticed them the first day in the shop—small-boned as birds, and pale, with black hair sprouting along the backs of the fingers. She had watched him brush them clean from the tobacco, and then count through his money like a spider. And she could see how they would mottle with age, how he would age himself—spry, sharp, sober.

"If I can get the motorcar, we can go for a drive," he said. "When shiveh is over."

"It's over now."

He turned to see how she meant him to take this, but she was staring soberly into the dark tangle of vines that covered the pillars of the summerhouse. "I want to learn how to drive a motorcar," she said. "I want to be able to drive myself wherever I want to go."

"If I can get the motorcar—" he began again.

But she stood up and turned to face him. "Get it next Sunday," she said. "We can go for a picnic."

HE CAME FOR HER after breakfast. Several times, as they drove through town and onto the coastal road, he tried to tell her with what difficulty he had acquired the use of the motorcar. But she had a way of interrupting that left him groping to get back to the subject. What he wanted her to know was that he had fought for her, that he had stormed and threatened in a way quite new to him. There was still the taste of sickness in his mouth, and pain, real pain across his heart. But she had rolled down the window, and was hanging her head out into the wind. She was laughing as the hairpins loosened and flew away, and her black hair streamed out in a wild river behind her.

"Which way?" he shouted, hesitating when they reached the coastal road.

"Up or down, I don't care."

He drove along the beachfront and then north over the bridge and across the lagoon. When they emerged onto the north coast road, she rested her chin on her arms and stared out at the sparkling immensity of the sea. It seemed to rise in an arch towards the horizon. There were boats out there, and a few ships waiting to go into the harbour. They were like flashes on the surface, hardly there if she widened her eyes. If Albert lost the careful grip he had fastened around the steering wheel and they slipped down into the water, the sea would simply close over them and go on like this forever, stretching away and away to all the other places in the world. And, oh, how Irma longed to be in all those other places.

When she had told her mother that she was going out for a picnic with Albert Kessel, Flora Gershin had given out one of her derisive laughs. "That *menuvel?*" she had said. "That laughingstock?"

Irma had laughed too. And yet, at the same time, a knot of bitterness had begun to tighten in her throat. She had known, of course, that her mother would scoff—she had counted on her scoffing. But now, looking at the old woman's ugly teeth bared, and the thick, moist tongue rising in derision, Irma found it hard to breathe.

"Even that father of yours would have laughed," Flora Gershin said, shaking her head. "Albert Kessel! Ha!"

Irma tossed her lovely head. "He's getting his mother's motorcar," she said. "I told him we're not sitting shiveh for a man like my father."

Her mother had sat up then and cocked her head like a bird. "That you should not have said, Irma." She rose, and went through to the kitchen, put some water on to boil the eggs. She sliced the last of the tongue for sandwiches, she cut the crusts off the bread as Irma always asked her to. She cut the sandwiches into quarters, packed them neatly in shredded lettuce, wrapped them in a damp serviette so that they would not dry out. They sat now in a basket on the back seat of Minnie Kessel's motorcar.

Albert tapped her on the shoulder. "Where would you like to stop?" he shouted. They had reached a crossroad through the sugarcane, and could either veer down to the beach, or drive on for another ten miles until they reached Port Salisbury.

Irma uncurled herself and sat up. She lifted her arms behind her and breathed in the leather and oil and metal of the hot car. "Turn here," she said. "We'll sit on the rocks."

SHE WATCHED HIM eat her mother's sandwiches, holding them delicately and leaning over so that nothing could fall onto his shirt. He had also rolled up his socks and placed them in one shoe, and then parked both shoes in the shade of the rock behind them. Irma closed her eyes, trying to remember the girl who had run off and left him. But every thought now only twisted itself into a vision of her mother—her large hands slicing the tongue, the terrible set of her jaw.

Until today, it had always been her father's fault. If there had been a fight between her parents, her mother would wait for him to leave the house before she would push herself out of her chair, and climb the stairs, and lock the bedroom door behind her. When he came home, he would have to try the handle again and again before he understood. *"You dried up hen!"* he would bellow. *"You diseased old sow!"* And then he would lurch down the passage to the divan in the sewing room. Never, on nights like that, had he come into Irma's room.

"In three months," said Albert, "I will be qualified." He had knotted his handkerchief to cover his head, but the wind kept lifting it off and so he had to hold it there with one hand and eat his hardboiled egg with the other.

Irma leaned back against the rock. The shade in which she sat smelled of stale seawater and rotting fish. "Come here," she said. *"Come here!"* she shouted over the roar of the surf and the squealing of the children in the water.

He took his handkerchief in his hand and crawled across the rock to her like a crab.

"One day," Irma said, pointing to a ship on the horizon, "one day I want to go away on a ship."

If Albert Kessel could have found the words, he would have told her right then that he would give her anything she liked. But being so close to her terrified him into silence. Everything about Irma Gershin terrified him, even her youth. He was young himself, and yet, with Irma, he felt as if he was already in a future still to be lived, with nothing to look back on, nothing to hope for either.

She sat up and took his hand in hers, turned it over as if to examine his palm. Then she bent her head and began to lick at it like a cat. She slipped her tongue between his fingers, looking up at him as she did this. He tried to smile, but it was impossible. And then, the next thing, she was pulling his hand, still wet with spittle, into her blouse. She slipped it under her bodice and left it on her breast, startled and rigid. "Do you love me, Albert?" she was shouting at him. "*Do* you?"

He nodded, he could do nothing else. With his hand still in place, she unbuttoned her blouse and loosened her bodice. And then she was bare to the waist in broad daylight, with people down on the beach and the tide coming in all around them. He glanced behind him, hoping that she would understand. But she only laid herself back against the rock and lifted one knee, so that he could see a little of the inside of her thigh.

He stared down at his hand, abandoned now, and longed to wipe it off on his trousers. But she was watching him. She had rolled her blouse and bodice into a pillow, and she lay there waiting, her eyes very black in the shadow.

"Irma," he said, "not yet. Not here. *Please!*"

Irma linked her hands behind her head and smiled. "Did you do it with her?" she asked. The thought was wonderful to her. Over the weeks, she had turned it into a sort of love story, a sort of lullaby in the dark of her room at night.

Albert pushed himself away from her. The smell and the fright had turned the sandwiches and boiled egg to vomit in his throat. "Irma," he said, "I wanted to marry you. I *want* to marry you."

He watched miserably as she sat up and reached behind her for her clothes. She would not look at him. She stared past him as she buttoned herself up, out at the ships on the horizon. What did she want from him, this strange, wild girl? His mother had asked him that this morning, and he had answered her with blame and hateful things. But really, what did Irma want? Why would she want to tempt him into danger in a place like this?

FOR A WEEK, NEITHER Irma nor Albert could talk to their mothers. Both women were practised in silence. They had used it on their husbands, closing themselves so solidly into it that even when they were ready to talk, it was hard to come out. But now, in both houses, the silence had begun to frighten them. It grew around them like a threat for the future—themselves left behind, old and sick, with no one to care about them, no one to blame for it either.

Even so, Albert's mother would not bring him his tea while he studied. Going down to the kitchen to fetch it for himself, he stepped carefully in his slippers so as not to wake her up. And all this because of Irma. When he thought of her, he lost sight of the future completely. All he could think was that, when he got the motorcar again, he would take her wherever she wanted to go, do whatever she wanted him to do, anywhere she liked. But how would he get the motorcar from his mother now? How would anything ever be the same again?

And then, on Friday, just as Irma was closing the shop, an Englishman walked in. "Would you have any idea where I can find a room for the weekend?" he said. "The hotels down here are full and I'm afraid I don't know where else to look."

He was red-faced and untidy in the heat, with a large suitcase, and a leather satchel over his shoulder. Irma let him watch her as she went about her closing up. And then, when she was ready to leave, she turned to him. "There's a room at my house," she said. "We will have to go on the tram."

Flora Gershin rose from her chair when she saw the stranger walk in with Irma. "Irma!" she cried. "What is this?"

Irma smiled. She took her mother's arm as if nothing had ever happened between them, and led her off toward the kitchen.

"What do you mean, a room?" Flora Gershin said, looking back over her shoulder at the man. "Tell him we don't rent rooms here. No."

But he was a headmaster, Irma explained. On Monday he would be going inland, to his school. And he would pay her whatever she asked, what was wrong with that?

Flora Gershin planted her feet and looked Irma in the eye for the first time in almost a week. "Tell the girl to put

sheets on the divan in the sewing room," she said. "And
to lay for him at supper. He wants supper with us, this
mister?"

During supper, Flora Gershin did not take her eyes
off Irma. The girl moved like a dancer from the sideboard
to the table. When she ate, she lifted her eyes to the
stranger. She asked softly whether he wanted more soup.
More fish? She was an actress, this girl, she was a dancing
girl and a whore, and Flora Gershin wanted to get up
from the table and take her in her arms herself.

But she didn't. She rose from her chair and went to
bed. There she lay for a long time, listening to them talk,
listening for them on the stairs, and then on the landing,
and then down the passage to the sewing room. After they
had closed the door, she fell into an easy sleep, a great
weight lifted off her heart.

THE SEWING ROOM was still rank with the smell of Irma's
father, and now it smelled of the Englishman too. Irma
lay beside him on the divan, trying to understand his
hands on her skin, his lips, his tongue. But in the dark of
the small, hot room, there was no form to what was happening, nothing but a dream of a dream of a dream. Only
when they finally lay back, and he began to whisper to her
in his strange, rich voice, did she remember who he was.
And then it was as if she were rising above them both—
rising so high that she could look down and see herself far

below. There she was, a small dark shape stretched out like a star. And everything around her was beautifully bright and blinding.

What loveliness, the Englishman was saying. What utter, utter loveliness.

Irma smiled into the dark. She could hear the sough of her mother's snoring, and Albert Kessel saying, Not yet, not here! She knew how to drive, her father had taught her on Sunday afternoons in Uncle Leon's motorcar. He had driven her up the coast and into the cane, and there he had sat her on his lap and let her steer the car anywhere she liked. He had shown her the gears, too, and explained about the pedals. But, with his hands over hers, his breath in her ear, she had pretended not to understand.

She sat up to go, but the Englishman held her back. "Let me look at you once more," he whispered. He stood up and switched on the lamp. And then he stared down at her for a long, long time. "What providence led me into your shop this afternoon?" he murmured. "Do you understand it? Do you?"

She shrugged. The Englishman would go off to his school, and she would either marry Albert Kessel or she wouldn't. She gathered up her clothes and walked, naked, to her room.

ON SUNDAY, WHEN Albert Kessel arrived at the front door, Flora Gershin had the pleasure of informing him that Irma was out. She had to say it twice before he would believe her. And still he stood there on the doorstep, staring at her like a startled hen. Soon enough he would hear, she thought, watching him down the steps. People would see the girl walking along the beachfront with that stranger, they would run with the news to Minnie Kessel.

And she was not wrong. The next evening, Minnie Kessel brought Albert his tea as usual. She put down the glass and folded her arms. "So," she said. "Be glad for yourself."

All night, Albert lay in the dark without sleeping. But when he arrived in the shop the following afternoon, Irma was there, exactly as before. He waited while she served the men who had come in before him. And then, when his turn came at last, she looked up at him and nodded.

"Irma—" he said. But nothing he had planned to say seemed possible now. "Irma?"

She unhooked a duster from the wall and began to wipe the counter from side to side.

He stared at the damp half circles under her arms. It was hot in the shop, his own shirt was sticking to him. "Irma," he said, "I'll get the motorcar this Sunday."

But that evening, when he asked his mother, she just put on her hat and took her bag and went off in the motorcar herself.

She drove to Flora Gershin's house, and rang the bell. And then, when the talk of the dowry was behind them, she left as quickly as she could.

Flora Gershin sat back in her chair and watched her daughter at the window. There had always been this separation to the girl, this beautiful, strange, dark stillness. She watched her as a man might watch her, trying to see what he might see. But now, waiting for Irma to turn back into the room, the stillness began to frighten her. Surely the girl knew that that *menuvel* would come for her anyway, dowry or no dowry? And, after all, would that be such a terrible thing? They could live in this foul house, all three of them together, and when Minnie Kessel came to visit, she would have to ring the doorbell like anyone else. "Irma," she said, "turn to your mother."

But Irma, watching Minnie Kessel climb into her motorcar, was already seeing Albert Kessel standing on the dock, his hair blown into a ridiculous halo by the wind. She saw him pass the shop, and stop to look in through the glass door, and drive the coastal road to the place they had gone for the picnic. He would walk down to the rock, perhaps. He would even come to the house and look up at this window as if she might still be here. She saw Albert Kessel, and she saw herself, as if already she were living the other girl's life.

Family of Shadows

At FIRST, PEOPLE SAID THAT PAULINE WAS THE WAY she was because Alma Cohen had strapped herself into a corset for her oldest son's bar mitzvah. But then later, when theories shifted, they put Pauline's strangeness down to the fact that the child had been so very unwanted from the start. Even Tobias Cohen himself did not come through unblamed. An upright man, whose steady rise to middling consequence had laced his cup with pride, he had considered his youngest daughter's peculiarities as an affront of Fate, had had her kept out of his sight, had waited years before calling in the doctors.

As it happened, no doctor could ever put a name to Pauline's state of mind. Governesses found that she could learn long passages of Wordsworth and Tennyson and Keats by heart, that she loved the Brontës and Jane Austen. She also read music, played the piano and the violin—but wildly, without care. Certainly, she didn't suffer the sort of madness that required drugs or incarceration. It was more like ungovernable eccentricity—comments out of the blue, sudden frowns, shrieks of laughter.

As soon as she was old enough, Tobias Cohen sent Pauline to live four hundred miles away, near her older sisters. Both sisters had married prominent captains of industry. They lived in big houses, with children, dogs, pools and tennis courts.

Pauline was set up in a small flat near some shops and the bus line. She even found herself a job as an usherette for the civic orchestra, bought herself a black dress, and mastered the seating pattern of the hall. But then, sitting at the back to listen, she would tap people on the shoulder and tell them to stop unwrapping sweets. Or she herself would hum along, or tap the floor, or both. If someone turned to scold her, she would put her finger over her lips and say, "Shoosh!" She seemed to understand quite clearly that there were things she did that annoyed or amused other people. But, annoyed herself by the brasses coming in too soon, or by "con brio" played "andante," she couldn't stop herself from standing up and shouting, "No!" Or from clapping her hands over her head and moaning if the soloist missed a note. So, they had to let her go.

But then she simply bought herself a season ticket, arriving early with her knitting. Pauline knitted for her nieces and nephews. The garments, however, always turned out stretched and grubby, and were passed on to the servants' children. The nieces and nephews themselves, once they were old enough to understand how things stood, made fine sport of Pauline. When she came for lunch on a Sunday, they would swoop in, draped in sheets, pretending to be ghosts. Or put a pooh-pooh cushion on her chair. Or crawl under the table and swipe her shoes. Half the fun was not knowing how Pauline would take it. Sometimes she would just say, "Oh, come on children, come off it!" But at others, she might tip her chair over backwards in terror. Or screech with laughter. Or scream so loudly that her brothers-in-law would slam out of the room in disgust.

Neither of her sisters did much to stop the play. Perhaps they did not want a revolution on their hands. As it was, their children quite looked forward to Pauline's visits. And their husbands used Pauline to bargain things for themselves. It was as if they had married down, to women who would need to make up the difference between their own and other normal families the husbands might have married into.

Every Christmas, when the sisters and their families went to the mountains for their holidays, Pauline went down to the coast. When Tobias Cohen was still alive, she had stayed with her brother and his family, provided sport for his children there. Now that Tobias was dead, however, there seemed no obstacle to her really going home.

TEA ON THE VERANDAH was strangely quiet. Pauline sat carefully at one end of the wicker couch with her cup and saucer, as if she were applying for a job. Alma Cohen noticed that she had grown portly over the past year. Her dress pulled at the seams, her breasts and stomach bulged. And her hair was beginning to grey. It stood out in a bonnet of fine fuzz that seemed to have receded from her forehead, giving her face the same rounded beaked look as Tobias Cohen's.

"After you've unpacked, perhaps we should go to town," Alma Cohen suggested. "You could probably do with some new clothes."

The morning was already steaming. There were hours left till lunch, days and nights and weeks to go before the trip back to the station.

Pauline grinned. "Ask your mother for sixpence to see the new giraffe, with pimples on his whiskers and pimples on his—" She snorted, spilled the tea at last, clattering cup and saucer back onto the tray and then standing up to shake out her skirt. "Sorry!" She covered her mouth, and guffawed again. "I want to go to the beach," she announced. "After lunch."

But after lunch, when Alma had gone off for a rest, Pauline settled onto the floor with the old photograph albums. Every Christmas, she asked for an afternoon with the albums, and every year it was arranged. The collection started with her parents' honeymoon and moved on—first born, second born, et cetera, the number of pages for each child diminishing in the usual way, down to nothing but a casual presence in the background for Pauline. The backgrounds themselves, in fact, were so shadowy that Pauline had to slide her glasses down her nose and peer closely to make herself out at all. This time, however, she didn't peer. She flapped through the pages, stopping deliberately with an "Ah!" to pull a photograph from its corners and tuck it under her thigh.

Alma woke with a start to the thought of beach sand tracked through the house. She called down to the kitchen, only to hear that Miss Pauline had never gone out at all, that she was in her room. Alma went to the room and tried the handle.

"Pauline!" she said. "Open this door at once!"

But Pauline was singing, rumbling around in there. Spilling the tea that morning had somehow returned her to herself. She had marched off to reacquaint herself with the house, moving from room to room, opening cup-boards, sniffing jars on her mother's dressing table, pounc-ing on a plate of jam squares in the pantry and stuffing two into her mouth. The servants watched with blank faces, giving nothing away. But, when she sat down at the piano and found the cover locked as usual, thumped two fists down hard, and then lifted the lid, sending a vase of lilies crashing to the floor—then the cook, fearing that she herself would somehow be blamed, ran out into the garden to tell the Madam.

"Pauline! I'll give you three! One! Two—"

The key turned in the lock. The trick had always worked. Alma closed her eyes. She would never get used to this, never. The door pulled wide, and there, in the middle of the room, stood Pauline in a pair of shoes, nothing else. She held a tuning fork in one hand, her violin in the other. Music was propped up against the dressing table mirror.

"Where is your dress, Pauline?" Alma asked, closing the door behind her. "For God's sake, consider the servants."

Pauline smiled. "Oh, Mater!" she said, using the same voice that her nieces and nephews used on her. "I undress to practise, didn't you know?" She pirouetted on the spot. Flakes of white shoe polish floated to the carpet. "Mrs. Molarsky says it frees the astral spirit."

Alma remembered now, with a surge of disgust, that it had always been difficult to keep clothes on Pauline. Even as a grown girl, she had had a childlike fascination with her body and its functions, particularly menstruation. "Bang on time this month!" she would announce in triumph to anyone at all. More than once, she had been caught peering at postcards of naked women, tilting them up to the light for a better look. No one knew where she had got them, where she had hidden them either. When, later, she reported in triumph to her sister that she had "done it" with the bricklayer, she was taken immediately to a gynaecologist, warned of all the things that could happen to her, given a diaphragm and instructions. And now here she was, unregenerate at thirty-five years old, her stomach and bottom bulging low and wide, black hair curling down in a dark streak from her navel. Even the room smelled rank with her sweetish-sour animal odour. Alma Cohen held her dressing gown close around her neck. "I'm going to get dressed for tea," she said.

Although the afternoon was hot and moist, Alma Cohen had all the doors and windows closed against the ghastly squawking and squeaking of Pauline's violin. It was Tobias who had loved music, particularly the violin. He would come home for lunch and put on a record, sit back and listen with a glass of tomato cocktail. And now this. Alma Cohen poured herself a cup of tea. She didn't miss Tobias, not as a husband, nor as a man. She had never even liked his music. What she missed was the daily assurance of his admiration. Other men, of course, admired her, even now, but their admiration was specific to her assets. Tobias Cohen, by contrast, had seen in his wife the paragon of womanhood. No other woman, not even his own daughters, could come anywhere near what Alma represented to him. She was as perfect as Pauline was imperfect. How many times had she heard him reiterate the irony of this? The one he chose; the one he didn't choose.

PAULINE CLATTERED IN with the evening paper. "You don't want the crossword puzzle, do you, Mater?"

"I never do the crossword puzzle."

"Good." She settled into the rocker, her glasses down her nose.

"But I'd appreciate a look at the headlines, Pauline," Alma said. She saw that the paper was already a mess. Tomorrow, she thought, she would order doubles for the month. It would save her peace of mind.

Pauline looked up, frowning. "Mater, can I have the driver tonight?"

"What did you have in mind?"

She closed her eyes and scratched her scalp. "Or I could catch the bus."

"You will certainly not catch a bus. How late do you plan to be out?"

"Not late."

And so the driver was summoned and told to have the car ready after supper. And, after supper, Pauline, in a black taffeta dress with a bright pink rose at the neckline, rode off into the night.

THE NEXT MORNING, Alma Cohen lay on the chaise in her bedroom with the Sunday papers and the coffee tray at her side. Barely a day had passed, and already her life seemed over in the way it had seemed over from the start with Pauline. Both of her older daughters had phoned that morning to find out how she was coping; both had roared at the news—obtained from Jedediah, the driver—that Pauline had spent the evening at the Lonely Hearts Club. Alma smiled, despite the frisson of pain behind her right ear, the beginning of one of her tension headaches.

"Mater!" The door burst open. Pauline stood before her in a skirted floral swimsuit. "Troubles come not single-handed!"

Alma stretched her neck back over the chaise. "What's the matter now, Pauline?"

"The curse is come upon me! I'm in full flood!"

"Do you need Kotex?"

Pauline smiled indulgently. "Mater, sometimes you really are thick, you know?" She flopped onto the bed and sank her head into her hands. "I know!" she said, suddenly. "May I bring him home for lunch?"

"HIM" TURNED OUT to be Stanley Teichelbaum, who was, if not quite a dwarf, certainly a halfwit. He was shorter than Pauline, with a huge forehead that sloped back sharply from his eyebrows and large, meaty ears. His hair was stringy and sparse, some teeth were missing towards the back, his arms were too short for his body, and his fingernails were long and dirty. Certainly his was not the sort of ugliness that Alma Cohen imagined would be exciting to a woman, not even to Pauline.

And yet there was Pauline, mute, squashing the tips of her fingers into her serviette ring.

"Pauline, did you have a nice time on the beach?" Alma asked.

Pauline slammed the serviette ring down on the glass-topped table. "I am *not* a child!" she shouted. "Kindly do *not* treat me like a child!"

Alma turned quickly to Stanley. Pauline's tantrums had always been best averted by changing the subject. But Stanley was pushing himself to his feet now. He stood facing Pauline with his shoulders back and his arms stiff at his sides. Then he opened his mouth and began to sing in a surprisingly full, deep baritone. "You are—"

Pauline's jaw fell open. As he sang on, she tilted her head this way and that like a dog, letting her tongue loll along her lower lip. Even when the song was over, she stared at him, frowning, as if she were trying to understand. But just as Alma Cohen reached for the bell to ring for soup, Pauline pushed her chair back and jumped to her feet. She clapped her hands to her cheeks and shouted, "Oh, *BRAVO*, Stanley! *BRAVISSIMO*, Stanley!"

Stanley blushed, giving a small bow in place. He pulled a grey handkerchief out of his pocket and wiped it around his head. "By trade," he explained to Alma, "I repair shoes. But I sing all the time. Everyone knows that I sing all the time."

Shoe polish. Alma realised she had smelled it the minute he walked in. She watched him tucking his serviette into his pants, prodding it in along his belt with stubby thumbs. In the strangest way, she would have quite liked to watch him fixing shoes. Despite her headache, she felt herself on the brink of laughter at the thought, the sort of mad, capricious laughter that afflicts people in school or church or bed. "You have a charming voice," she said.

"'She has a lovely face; God in his mercy lend her grace, The Lady of Shalott.'" Pauline cupped a hand and gave Stanley a little wave. He waved back.

Alma rang the bell for soup. It was no coincidence that Pauline caused scenes when there was someone there to witness them. Tobias had always said she was canny in this way. On occasion, it had even been pleasant for Alma to raise her voice on Pauline's behalf, if only to have Tobias say, "You, my dear, cannot possibly understand the workings of such a mind." As if Pauline were a common tart, a thief, a murderess.

"Mater, where's the key to the piano?"

Stanley bent low over his soup bowl, blowing in quick, short blasts.

"The soup is chilled," Alma said. "It's cucumber."

Pauline leaned across the table. *"Where's the key, Mater?"*

"I put it somewhere. Hmm." Alma pretended to think. But she wanted to slap Pauline's big, fat face; she wanted to sink ten fingers into that hideous hair and pull it out by the roots.

"*I* know!" Pauline said to Stanley. "After lunch, we can have a treasure hunt!"

Alma stood up. The sinews in her neck stretched tight against her skin. The skin itself had long since lost its matte olive glow. It looked sallow now, dry as tissue. "You will do no such thing, Pauline," she said slowly. "You and your visitor may finish your lunch. And then please try to be quiet while I'm resting. I have a headache."

She heard them giggling as she left the room, the tart and her idiot, and a knot swelled in her throat. By the time she locked herself into her bedroom, she was gasping for breath. She lay across the bed and tried to cry, but all she could think of was Pauline coming home year after year, now that there was no one to stop her. All these years, Alma Cohen had allowed people to believe that it was Tobias alone who had stood between Pauline and visits home. Not that she had pretended any enthusiasm herself, but that she had encouraged—by the sort of wifely silence she kept on the subject—a suspicion that she might have had it otherwise.

Downstairs, they were moving about. She heard the tuning fork bing and his voice start up again. "You are——"

There were a lot of things, Alma Cohen realised, that she had accomplished with silence. Even pleasure. Standing in a satin nightdress in front of her long dressing table mirror, she had liked to have Tobias come up behind her, to have him ask her, once again, how he had come to deserve such good fortune. To this she had never given an answer. But now, going over the question, she wished she had mentioned how much she detested the smell of tomato cocktail on his breath, and the sough of his breathing at night, his hairs in her hairbrush.

She reached for the house phone and ordered tea on

the verandah. Then she sat at the dressing table, fingering some rouge into the hollows of her cheeks, touching up her lipstick and her hair. At sixty-nine—still handsome, with that careful elegance of dress that had always distinguished her from the other *arrivistes* of her set—she knew that good things had always come her way when she didn't step out of character. Passion, for instance, would never have suited her. Once or twice, when it had brushed her lightly—always in the voice of adoration—she could have stumbled, brought her world down around her ears. Even now, when she widened her large, dark eyes, turned her face at an angle, people thought of Garbo smouldering. There was still something in the hotness and coldness of her that had the little Portuguese vegetable man growling, "Oh lady, lady, lady, I lôve you, lôve you, lôve you!"

The singing had stopped. The tea tray rattled through. A door slammed. Passing Pauline's room on her way downstairs, Alma heard the shoe man shouting, *"Oh no!"* and Pauline's lunatic laugh—the screech, the wheeze, the grunt. Alma stopped, closed her eyes to steady herself. And then she knocked.

The door cracked open, and Pauline thrust her head out. "Oh! Mater! Say not the struggle naught availeth!"

"Pauline, I'd like a word with you, if you please."

"Can't. I'm measuring."

"You're what?"

Pauline fluttered a tape measure in Alma's face. She

opened the door a little to reveal Stanley Teichelbaum standing soberly behind her, stripped to the waist. His flesh was pale as dough, and hairy, with small flaps of breast. Alma Cohen quickly looked away.

"He won't stay *still*," Pauline complained. "What do you think, Mater? Maroon or bottle green?"

"I've never gone in for bottle green," Stanley said, coming forward. "I told her that, but she won't listen."

Alma Cohen forced herself to look over his head and into the room. The bed was still made. The curtain voiles billowed in the afternoon breeze. Snapshots had been stuck all around the mirror. One came unstuck and fluttered to the floor. "Kindly tell me," she said at last, "what all this is about?"

"She's knitting me a pullover," Stanley said.

Pauline roped the tape measure around his neck and drew him back into the room. "Come into the garden, Maud, For the black bat, night, has flown."

"Oh *no!*" he shouted.

SITTING ALONE ON THE verandah, watching the city shimmer in the afternoon heat, Alma Cohen thought she might just tell Pauline she could either move over to her brother's or go home altogether, but here she could not stay. It was all very well for the girls to find the Lonely Hearts Club amusing, but it was she, Alma, who had to bear the brunt of the madness, think up threats that could be brought to bear. Tobias had had no such trouble, not even when Pauline was a child. At the sound of his car up the hill, his key in the door, she had jumped up and clattered out of the room, off to the kitchen to find her nanny. It was then—the flush of terror in the girl's face, the terrified impulse to obey—that a small ache could take hold of Alma Cohen's heart, make her consider calling Pauline back. But she never had. And now nothing seemed clear—past, present, future. Where did childhood end?

The French doors burst open and there they stood. "Mater," said Pauline, "kindly come forth with the piano key! Pronto!"

Alma Cohen reached for her bag. More and more, Pauline looked like Tobias—the bulgy stare, the neck sunk low into the shoulders.

"I'm no good without a piano," Stanley explained. His jaw hung slack, as if he had more to say. He ran his tongue along his lower lip.

"His mother used to play," said Pauline, snatching the key. "But now she's dead."

THERE WAS NOWHERE to go but out into the garden, and, even there, with the French doors open, Alma Cohen could hear every note, every word. She made her way down to the summerhouse, settled herself onto the bench there. It was years since she had gone this far into the garden. Usually, she ventured only onto the upper terrace, to instruct the gardener on what to pick for the house, where to weed, when to plant. Now, she looked out over the lawn, the hedge, the city beyond, and she felt as if she had landed in another country. Behind her, the house, with its white pillared verandahs and red tiled roof, could have been a ship docked for the day. The heavy scent of the frangipanis was like the breath of another life.

"You are——"

WHEN PAULINE MARRIED Stanley Teichelbaum four months later, people said it was a pity Tobias Cohen had not lived to have to face what others had to face in their lives one way or another. A wedding he could not have ignored. And this one had even made it into the papers when the Lonely Hearts Club, learning of Pauline's connections, demanded more than their usual fee for the match, and the captains of industry sued.

After the wedding, the couple moved inland, back to Pauline's flat. Stanley Teichelbaum gave up mending shoes and took a job as a foreman in his brother-in-law's warehouse. Pauline promised her sisters that she would take her birth control pills every day, but, when she forgot and fell pregnant, she refused to have an abortion. The son that was born to Pauline and Stanley was quite normal. Better than normal, really, he was quick, passionate to learn, and gifted with natural charm. In the way that such things happen, he was also beautiful. He had a head of thick, curly hair, wide, dark eyes, and matte olive skin.

Pauline and Stanley never questioned their good fortune. They loved their son as they loved each other—in a noisy disorder of glee and generosity. When he grew old enough to have their measure, it caused him no embarrassment. On the contrary, he would place himself between his parents and those who might ridicule them. And so, on his account, they became less ridiculous.

It was only Alma Cohen that the boy could not abide. When she called him over to ask about school or games—to look at him really, the loveliness of his face and figure—he pretended not to hear her. If she came to him, he squirmed away with excuses. Nothing she could offer him brought him willingly to her side.

When Pauline and her family came down to the coast for the holidays and Alma Cohen invited friends for tea, people noticed the boy's aversion. It served her right, they said. All her life Alma Cohen had held herself aloof from life's surprises. Who did she think she was? Who was she, after all?

An Error of Desire

IF IT WEREN'T FOR THAT LITTLE LEG OF HERS, ONE would have said Charlotte was throwing herself away on Colin McKenzie. She was a better class of person altogether—better spoken, better educated, far more intelligent, and, if one could overlook that leg, rather appealing in an old-fashioned sort of way. Still, there she was, limping up the aisle on his arm, affecting a rather superior sneer so that anyone might know that this was not the happiest day of her life.

Well, not exactly anyone. Eileen was there, wearing her customary uniform—trousers and rubber sandals, and her thick hair shaved up her neck. Charlotte had told her not to come, but of course she came anyway. Had she ever paid any attention to Charlotte's wants or needs?

When I first questioned Charlotte about Eileen, she just shrugged, the little leg kicking under her skirt. It had a way of kicking like that when something amused her, or when something upset her. It was the reason I'd had to move her out of the Juniors and into the Intermediates. Mothers had complained. It was frightening for children to see that little leg, they said, bound up as it was in one long, brown leather thong.

The first time Charlotte limped into my office, applying for the position of Junior Voice Coach, I hardly had time to notice the contraption on her leg before she began telling me the story of it. She had been born normal, she said—crawling, standing and so forth. But then, just when she was beginning to walk, her right leg stopped growing from the knee down. And so there it was now, one haunch shrivelling down into a baby's leg, with a baby's foot wriggling at the end of it.

"Apart from anything else," I said, "Eileen doesn't look clean."

"*Clean?*"

"Her fingernails and so forth."

Charlotte laughed. I suppose she thought I would understand the appeal on a broader front than fingernails. But she was wrong. I had never understood it. How did it happen, woman for woman? Where was the heart of it? Men, yes—I could understand that—even the lowest of them, even the beggars on the street. When, occasionally, I myself would thrill to the thought of them burdened by desire, I was always glad for the silence of the mind and heart. What would the mothers of the Juniors have to say about this? Iris Ballin, principal of The Ballin Studio of Speech and Drama, thrilling herself with the thought of a beggar? Ha!

"The thing is," Charlotte said, "I just can't help it."

They all said this, men and women both, and I believed them. And yet, with Charlotte, I couldn't help putting it down to that little leg of hers. I would have said that it had made her shy with men, except that Charlotte wasn't shy with anyone. If her brace hurt her, she would simply unbuckle it and take it off, right there, in front of the class, exposing the bound-up thing itself.

One day she even held it out to me. The foot needed manipulation, she said, starting to unwrap the leather thong. But the sight of that foot sent me fussing for the phone book, looking up the address of St. Bartholomew's Hospital. And yet I had never been squeamish about the foot before. On the contrary, I had always found myself drawn to it. It was grotesque—pink and soft, and it seemed to have a life of its own, like a small animal. Still, I had never wanted to touch it. I couldn't bear the thought of touching it.

I gave her the address of St. Bartholomew's, and she went the next afternoon. And that is where she found Eileen.

Eileen is a physiotherapist. One can only imagine how she used her skills to move on from whatever it was that she was doing to that foot of Charlotte's, to getting her to leave her flat on the ridge and come down to the beachfront to live with her. Every morning, hot or cold, rain or shine, she led Charlotte, hopping, across the beach and into the surf. And then they swam out together, beyond the waves, right up to the shark nets.

"It's dangerous," I said, when Charlotte told me. "What if you went too far? What if some urchin made off with your brace?"

Charlotte laughed. She was so happy with that creature that everything, even danger, seemed to delight her. Watching her like this, I found myself forgetting for a minute that Eileen was not a man. Certainly, I could understand the delight itself, I could even envy it—the way it rings one around, closing out all common sense, closing out everything but the present happiness.

And yet Eileen was as grim as a person could be. Every afternoon, she turned up at the studio, stolid and unsmiling. She would sit in the vestibule, waiting for Charlotte to come through the door, all flourish and books, with the pupils crowding around her. And then she would get up and hold the front door open so that there was no question of Charlotte delaying with them or with me. If I wanted to speak to her, I had to come forward and say, "May I have a word with you please, Charlotte?" And then Eileen would roll her eyes and look at her watch and sigh.

After six months of this, Charlotte came up to the house one day, looking pale and gaunt and ruined. I showed her quickly into the study and closed the door. "What's the matter?" I asked her.

"We fight all the time," she said. "She's jealous. And she loves to make me jealous too."

"Jealous of *her?*" It seemed as impossible as the whole arrangement itself.

"She *enjoys* making me jealous," she cried. "I've never known anyone so cruel!"

"Charlotte," I said, "that creature has robbed you of your common sense. Just *look* at her!"

But nothing through my eyes made any sense to Charlotte. How could it? She was bewitched, she was enchanted by a gorgon. "Have you ever considered a man?" I asked.

She looked up, startled.

"Someone who might offer you the hope of a normal life," I said.

She snorted derisively, the leg kicked out. "For God's sake, Iris! I thought *you* of all people understood."

They all think this because I am so easy with their arrangements. Why wouldn't I be? I have always thought that they are born the way they are, poor devils, men and women both, they can't help it. When their arrangements fall apart, as they so often do, I am the one they come to. They arrive at the house, tear-streaked and miserable, and I show them right into the study, knowing exactly what I am in for. It is always the same—tales of woe, tales of blame and misery. And me thinking to myself, How does it happen? Where does it start—such an error of desire?

"Charlotte," I said, "don't think I don't know what it is to be miserable."

She frowned then. Toby and I are never allowed to let them down. And even if they think that, given half a chance, we'd be just like them, this is not what they want for us, not at all. And yet, if they really wanted to know, I could tell them how tiresome it can be, playing happy families for such an audience. And that there are moments, like now, when even I can feel the loss—the necessary loss, I suppose—of all my old happiness.

"Just consider what you might have to look forward," I said. I had been waiting for a chance to say this because, despite that leg, Charlotte was usually spirited and bright. And she could be lovely too. She had a sort of long-boned elegance that went well with her pale skin and that pale hair curling down her back. Even Toby was not above practising his charm on her. Surely, I would think, there must be some decent fellow somewhere in want of a young and grateful wife? "Don't rule out a man, Charlotte," I said. "You just never know who might come along, my dear."

AND THEN, AS IF I had wished him into existence, there at the bus stop, not two days later, was Colin, stopping to offer her a lift. Actually, he offered a lift to both women standing there, and even though the other woman turned him down, Charlotte got in. That was how she always was, careless with her safety, and I couldn't help admiring her for it. All my life I had prided myself on my common sense, and now here was this wild thing with a gammy leg, turning her unpromising life into an adventure.

The next morning, Colin was at the bus stop again. And the next again. And then every morning after that. When Eileen found out, she began her throwing—first, Charlotte's things out onto the street, and then Charlotte herself, right across the kitchen. She arrived at the studio with a cut on her forehead and an armful of clothes, and I said, "All right, enough, you'll come and stay with us for a while."

And so she did. It was like having an enormous child in the house, sullen and pouting. Toby began to pout, too, because she hardly noticed his existence. She hardly noticed anything, I pointed out, except the ringing of the telephone. When it rang, she would rear up from the table like a great sea beast and hurl herself across the dining room to the hall. But it was only Colin, it was always Colin. And back she would limp, looking as if she would burst into tears.

One afternoon, I came home to find her at the front door, bright and cheerful, with her suitcases packed beside her. "Don't scold me, Iris," she said, "Eileen's coming to fetch me."

"What about Colin?" Every day, he would come to the house to drive her down to the studio, and every lunchtime, there he was again, waiting to bring her home. "Charlotte," I said, "you can't just leave him in the lurch."

She laughed gaily. "Oh, Colin!" she said. "He'll just have to understand."

And so this is how it went on for almost a year. After a while, I had the house girl keep the bed in the spare room made up, ready for her next return. Sometimes Eileen would not even let her take her clothes with her, and I had to lend her this or that of my own. When Colin came to see me, to ask for my help, I could only shake my head.

"Colin," I said, "it's like a drug with these people. Can't you find yourself a normal sort of woman?"

But he didn't want a normal sort of woman; he wanted Charlotte. Perhaps the foot had done its work on him, too, how could I know? When I looked at him, all I saw was a man madly in love. There is love and there is desire, I thought, and for all the world they look the same until the desire is spent.

One day, Charlotte came into my study. She had been in the house longer than usual this time, and I thought she was coming to tell me that she was leaving again.

"He's asked me to marry him," she said, slumping into a chair. She was not cheerful, nor was she sullen. She simply sat there, waiting to see what I would say.

I knew what she wanted. She wanted me to urge her to accept, to point out that he would care for her, give her children, and a normal life. And then she would be able to argue with me. She would tell me that it was all very well for me, I had my marriage, my children, my career, but that for herself she wanted only to be free, to make her own choices and so forth.

I busied myself with the tea tray, saying nothing. If it were not for her affliction, I would have been tempted to tell her that I had always refused to lower my price because of a plain face and a difficult figure. And that if I had seemed to triumph in my husband, well one could, perhaps, do better than a vain, weak man who had been spoiled completely by the women in his life.

"There is one condition," she said with a laugh. "I am never to see Eileen again."

When I still said nothing, she looked down into her lap. "He said he would get me a car, equipped with a special accelerator. And then he would teach me to drive." She couldn't help a small smile of pride, although she tried hard to smother it. "Everything I have ever got, I got for myself," she said. "My mother never did a thing to help me."

It is always the mothers. Either they love them or they hate them, nothing in between.

"If I could bear the thought of it," she began, tracing the pattern in the brocade with her finger. Then she looked up, as if indeed we had been arguing. "Don't you think I might want a normal future for myself, too?" she demanded, the leg kicking out in a furious rhythm.

The gate slammed, Toby was back from the studio. All afternoon, he had been rehearsing the new Juliet, although there was no need.

"But Iris!" she cried suddenly, her eyes brimming. "Oh, Iris!"

I reached for her hand then and, holding tight, began to tell her what she had come to me to hear. I painted all the pictures I had painted for myself, the words fading into the silent room like smoke.

She did not let me finish. She shook herself free and struggled out of her chair. "It's okay," she announced, "I've made up my mind. I'm going to tell him tonight. I'm going to do it."

AND SO THERE SHE was, not three weeks later, affecting a grotesque sort of waltz with him around the studio auditorium. At least Eileen had the sense not to come there. I would have turned her away if she had. I'd had to arrange everything myself—food, flowers, guests. From the day she accepted him to the day of the wedding itself, Charlotte had been useless, lost in a cloud of unhappiness.

"Am I doing the right thing for her?" Colin had asked me a few days before the wedding. Charlotte was upstairs with a headache, and Toby, who had an aversion for any man a woman might prefer to himself, always refused to come home for dinner if Colin was going to be there. I was relieved. It was difficult enough getting Charlotte to be civil without having Toby snorting every time Colin had something to say.

"The right thing for *her*?" I said. "What about for yourself, my dear?"

But still he seemed to want an answer. He sat forward, blinking at me through his thick glasses. "I know, Mrs. Ballin, that I can give her a better life. She just needs time to forget that woman."

Perhaps it was then that I understood what might have been plain if only I had chosen to see it—that Eileen was all the life and the passion between him and Charlotte. Without Eileen, how could this careful, mumbling man have ever hoped to secure a woman like Charlotte, leg or no leg? Without Eileen, how would the marriage itself continue?

As if to answer this, Charlotte arrived at the house three months after the wedding. "Iris," she said, "may I come back here for a few days?"

"No, my dear," I said. "You have a husband now. Unless he is throwing you across the kitchen, which I very much doubt that he is—no."

She bowed her head, breathing deeply.

"Look," I said, "don't think I don't know how difficult it can be."

She nodded like a child. Even the leg was still for once.

"Charlotte," I said, "how are things in the physical department? With Colin I mean?"

At this she shook her head furiously. "I cannot *bear* it, Iris," she cried. "I cannot bear *it*. The only way I can get myself through it is to think of Eileen."

Ah, Eileen. Well, so what? I thought. Where was the harm in her being locked into Charlotte's heart and kept there, out of sight?

"I have to behave like a *criminal*," she wailed. "I have to lie and cheat and say that I'm teaching when I'm not."

"You are *seeing* that woman again?"

She stared at me. All her old defiance was gone, her face was white and streaked with tears.

"Oh, Charlotte!" I said. How could one cope with this obstinate woman bent on ruining the life she had just begun to make for herself? And yet, there was a frisson of delight in it, a frisson of relief as well. "If it's like this in the beginning," I said, "what hope can there possibly be for the future?"

"Oh, Iris!" She held out her arms to me, and I went over to her, clasping her close, like a child.

"Why not just give Colin back the car and the house," I said, "and move down to the beachfront, once and for all?"

She sat back then and groped into her pocket for a

hanky, blowing her nose furiously. "I'm going to have a baby, Iris," she said. "She won't have me back unless I get rid of it first."

THERE WERE TWO children before Charlotte finally moved out. And with each child, she become more bitter. "What I cannot *bear*," she would say, "is being locked into the house like a cow. I can't stand it, Iris—really, I can't stand any of it."

"*I* was never locked in," I said. "I was back at the studio three weeks after each child."

She shrugged. Coming back to the studio would solve nothing for her, I knew this. The problem was that she had lost her old hope for herself, she had left it behind with Eileen. She looked different now, too. Her hips had thickened, and she had cut her hair. It sprang out around her head in ringlets, giving her the look of a large, disconsolate child. Even the little leg was zipped into some sort of knitted arrangement, like a flesh-coloured Christmas stocking. To see Colin smiling at the sight of her, one child on her lap and the other twisting itself into her skirt, was to see a man who thought he had won the battle fairly.

"It's all very well for you," she said. "You had Toby."

I shrugged. Perhaps she had a point after all. For all his weakness, for all my scorn, still there had been those first moments between us—more than moments, years— that wonderful circle of happiness around us. And even when it left us, fading so slowly that we hardly seemed to notice the disappointment—even then there was the memory of it to make sense of the life that was to follow. What would we have been without it? Where would we both be now?

"I shall *die* if I have to go on like this, Iris," she said. "I'm not joking, I shall *die*."

THE DAY AFTER she left him, Colin came to the house. "What sort of a mother would do such a thing?" he demanded. "What am I supposed to say to the children?"

His jaw hung slack, and he had a way of pushing his tongue out over his teeth that revolted me completely.

"Why not tell them that she went to live with a woman?" I said.

"But that's the thing—she *didn't*. She's moved into the Admiral Hotel, down on the beachfront. If I want them to see her, I have to take them down there."

I had to swallow a laugh. There was a sort of lunatic pleasure at the thought of Charlotte refusing to budge from the Admiral.

"And then they just cry when I have to take them home," he said. "I mean, is it fair? What am I supposed to tell them?"

THE NEXT DAY, I went down to the Admiral myself. I found her sitting on the verandah of the hotel, watching the surf raging in over the sea wall.

"You haven't come to scold me, have you, Iris?" she said. The knitted stocking was gone, the leather thong too. I could see the whole little leg through the voile of her sundress. "It's spring tide," she said, "I dare not go in."

"Where's Eileen?" I asked.

"Eileen? She left the country ages ago."

"What about the children, Charlotte? I'm not scolding, I'm just asking."

But she only laughed at this, as if I had cracked a joke. "Iris," she said, "can you use me at the studio again?"

"I certainly can, my dear."

And so it was done. She stayed on at the Admiral. Colin gave her the car, and a small settlement of money. At first, he brought the children down to the hotel every weekend, but then he married again—such men always do—and, after that, the children didn't see Charlotte as regularly. She didn't seem to mind. She had never been much of a mother, and if they wanted to see her, all they had to do was to go down to the beach at five o'clock in the evening. There she was, rain or shine, lurching across the sand. When she reached the water, she sat down to unstrap and unbuckle the brace, and then, with fierce pleasure, she threw it up onto the beach.

Once, waiting for her there myself, I saw two girls sitting on the sea wall and knew they must be hers. One had Charlotte's hair, the other was dark, like Colin. They sat in silence, never taking their eyes off their mother. When she suddenly disappeared under a wave, the older one jumped up and pulled the other to her feet. They were about to leap onto the sand and run down into the surf themselves when Charlotte came up in the smooth waters beyond the waves, triumphant, blowing like a whale.

Liars, Cheats,
and Cowards

ALL MEN ARE LIARS. PSALM 116:11. OVER THE YEARS
I added "cheats and cowards" to round out the
phrase. "All men are liars, cheats and cowards" trips
nicely and has the sound of truth. It is a truth I began to
discover early, even though, back then, I still modified my
observations with hope.

What is odd is that most men seem to embrace the
liar-cheat-coward slur as a compliment. It's a sort of cow-
boy compliment, something out of the movies, almost as
if the ability to lie, cheat, and run away from danger
makes the assumption of romantic necessity. More than
this, there is the idea that the man himself is the sort who
can command such assumptions—that, for the sake of his
women, he has had to learn to lie, cheat, and, in extremis,
run for his life.

From the start it was clear to me that Ernest was different. He lied, of course, but his lies were about me.

They were the sort of compliments that a man in love makes to the woman he wants. Every now and then I would see him glance at other women. No man, I knew, not even Ernest, wanted one woman only. I myself wanted many, many men just as most men wanted many women. There was danger in this. I couldn't afford the luxury. And Ernest, for all his looking, was really a one-woman man. As my grandfather would have said about a sturdy, moderately priced shoehorn, Ernest was a good article.

Before I arrived in Boston, Ernest had gone about cutting off his relationships with other women in the same methodical fashion that he snipped off benign moles or cut out cysts. By the time my plane landed he was clean of all sordid connections. He found us a month-to-month furnished apartment and equipped it with hospital sheets and blankets and cutlery and crockery. It never occurred to me to consider him a thief in this. He let me drive his car. He asked me to marry him. I, caught between a future involving some husband or other and a present need for employment, said I'd consider the offer. He pressed for an answer. He wanted to tell his family, he said. I was to be offered up together with his certificate of specialization for a summer spectacular.

Dozens of times a day I considered Ernest as husband. People told me he was perfect for the role. Responsible. Dependable. Intelligent. Somehow, though, he seemed to have concluded, without my telling him, that I didn't much desire him as a lover. And so he considerately waited for me to be asleep before making love to me. This husbandishness troubled me a lot. I wanted to want him as I wanted other men, but, somehow, just as I'd be observing him hopefully from behind—his head bent, a large masculine arm resting like a lion on the formica table—he'd stab a finger onto a classified ad and look up over his glasses and ask, "Two bedroom, partial view?" And it would be gone.

Then, one evening, we were invited for coffee by a senior colleague and his wife, who had just had a baby. Ernest was excited by the invitation. It had the stamp of coupledom to it. I understood immediately that coffee without dinner was not much of a stamp. But still, I was curious to see whether people who were married and had a baby could seem happy.

The Shapiros certainly made a *thing* of being happy. They greeted us at the door with the sort of comradely whoops and halloos that the just-married use on the soon-to-be-wed.

"Welcome, welcome, welcome!" they said.

Ernest steered me into the apartment talking of "we" and "our." Lonnie, with the baby whinging over her shoulder, invited me to follow her into the kitchen. The men settled themselves into hospital talk in the living room. Coffee percolated cosily on the kitchen counter.

Lonnie reached into the freezer with one hand, holding the baby in place with the other, and pulled out a box of Pepperidge Farm apple turnovers. She struggled with the package.

"Here," I said, "let me."

The baby crossed its eyes and drooled and scrunched. Lonnie placed four frozen triangles neatly on the tray of a small square appliance nesting next to the percolator. She closed its door, moved a lever, pressed a bar, and called, *"Men!"*

The men took a while to come in. On the kitchen table she had laid out some of the spoils of her marriage— plasticized straw mats, stoneware plates and mugs, patterned forks and spoons in silver plate. I watched her, wondering about happiness. She grabbed up the apple turnover package and threw it into a garbage can under the sink. Then she winked at me and gestured towards the frozen triangles, sizzling now under a ray of red heat. "He thinks I make them myself," she said.

David Shapiro swaggered into the kitchen with Ernest behind him. Ernest made a show of lifting his nose into the air and patting his stomach. "Ah!" he said. He smiled at me and bent over to kiss my cheek "You okay?" he asked. He seemed very happy.

"Ever seen one of these?" David pointed at the small appliance with the apple triangles in it.

Ernest lowered his nose to counter height and crept

up with one hand on each knee. He took off his glasses and peered through the glass of the appliance door. He seemed to need time to decide whether he'd ever seen such a thing before. Then slowly he shook his head. "Nope," he said. "Never."

"It's a toaster oven!" Lonnie announced. She craned around the mound on her shoulder and winked at me again. "I don't know what I'd do without it."

Ernest turned and gestured silently for me to join him. "Come, babe," he said. "You've gotta have a look at this."

I went to stand behind him and listened in silence as Lonnie and David pointed out this and that. The toaster. The oven. The broiler. Boom, they said, all in one.

ON THE WAY HOME Ernest was ecstatic. "If we do it," he said to me, reaching over for my hand at a red light— "Mind you, I say *if*—we've gotta have one of those things."

"What things?" I asked. I could hardly breathe.

"That toaster oven. Hell! It's got everything. Oven. Broiler. It's compact. Uses less electricity. Say!" He slowed to a creep (he always had trouble divorcing the pace of his driving from that of his thinking). "Do you think we could spring your parents for one?" He even blushed. I saw a red ear under the passing glow of a streetlight.

I stared down at his hand on mine in silence. Happiness or no happiness, future, present, God knows what, I couldn't marry this man.

"I couldn't very well ask them how much it cost," he went on, "but how much could it be, for God's sake? Twenty? Thirty?"

I still had the return half of my airline ticket. I'd leave a note. No, I wouldn't. Cowards leave notes. I'd explain straight out. I'd use a man's excuse. "I'm no good for you. I'd be a lousy wife. I'm doing this for your sake." That would make me a liar. So, okay, I'd tell him I was doing it for my sake. I could say I had someone else, lie and say I couldn't stand the lies any more. Oh God. How would I do it? Just leave? Be gone by the time he returned from the hospital. A damned coward? No note, no nothing, the way men behaved? I looked at him.

He smiled back. "Remember G.E.," he said. "Dave says to settle for nothing but a G.E."

EIGHTEEN YEARS LATER our marriage foundered when Ernest discovered I had cheated. While I was visiting my parents thousands of miles away he brought up some burglary tools from the basement and broke into the locked file in my studio. There he found some love letters and a journal, and lots and lots of cuttings and clippings and notes that meant nothing to him. He phoned me, his voice triumphant across the continents and oceans, to announce that he wanted a divorce. "You're a liar," he said. "Start to finish."

Before I arrived home, Ernest had fled to visit his sister in Missoula. I had to wait three weeks before he would return to face the great divide.

ON THE LIST OF household items to be shared was the toaster oven. It still worked. Toaster. Broiler. Oven. Ernest, however, scanning the classified ads for somewhere to live, waved it away without looking up. Its appeal was lost. Replaced over the years by all those good articles of marriage—the electric knife, the Cuisinart, the coffee grinder, the microwave.

The Curse of the Appropriate Man

HALF A LIFETIME OF APPROPRIATE MEN CAN LEAVE a woman parched for adventure. Like someone who has never seen the sea, or heard a foreign language spoken on its native soil. Let other women scan the personals for a DWM, 50s, professional, nondrinker, nonsmoker—this woman wants anything but. She's had it with men who ask before they touch. She's reached the time in her life when she wants a man with a few bad habits. Something unexpected. A wrangler, a wrestler, even a racketeer will do. As for her future, she's got it on hold. For the moment, she wants to be surprised.

And then, one night, at an academic pot luck party, she meets a bearded Bavarian in the seventeenth year of his doctoral dissertation. His subject, he tells her, involves the dual fields of ecology and Chinese. For money, he plays the cello on a street corner—tourist stuff—and teaches archery at the local community college. His style of living, he says, is rather unusual. And would she like to come for dinner one night?

She finds her way, as instructed, to a rambling fake Tudor tenement near the university. It is, she has been told, the victim of a rent control standoff. The garden is overgrown and the doorbells don't work. She must tap out a particular rhythm of knocks to alert the Bavarian of her arrival.

Sure enough, he is at the front door in seconds and leading her into a large hall that is dim and damp and chill. It smells of must and old frying oil. Three or four bicycles are propped and chained to the banisters. The Bavarian himself is neatly tied and pinned into a waiter's apron. In one hand, he holds a large upholstery needle. "Permit me," he says, "to lead ze vay."

She follows him up two flights of stairs to what must once have been the servants' floor, and then to a door numbered "11"—neither here nor there in her bad luck category.

The room is small and oblong, no larger than a doctor's waiting room. But, with a ceiling almost as high as the room is wide, and a strange arrangement of furniture, it takes time for her to take it all in.

Along one wall is a single bed, disguised into a couch by a good Persian rug and kilim cushions. Above it hangs an enormous wooden bow and a quiver of arrows, a sepia photograph of a bearded soldier in a spiked helmet, and a few strangely shaped knives with ornate handles. A small desk takes up the corner opposite. It holds a gleaming antique typewriter, a few leatherbound books, and a bottle of ink. And, in the center of the room, a card table has been set for two—tablecloth, candles, wine glasses, the lot.

She accepts a glass of wine and is about to sit on the bed when she sees—suspended like a swing by two looped chains—a large piece of driftwood.

"Do you use this for exercise?" she asks, noticing, for the first time, how enormous he is—head and hands and feet, and all that hair.

He shakes his head soberly and lays down the needle, which he has threaded with a strip of glistening lard. He comes over, unhooks the swing and lets it drop. It hangs now just above the outer edge of the bed. In fact, it is more like a ladder than a swing. There are two more struts of driftwood at equal intervals, up to the ceiling.

"Ven I let it down," he explains, "zhis is zhe bedroom, ja? Ven I hook it back up, like so, it is zhe liwing room, ha?" He fixes her with a teacherly smile. "P-sychologically, you see, it is impôrtant to delineate."

Suddenly, she is lonely for the old life, for someone who would wonder where she is and come to look for her. But she settles herself onto the couch or bed, hoping that the dinner won't take long.

Bluebeard, however, doesn't even seem to have a

kitchen. There's no cooktop, no oven, no spoons or spatulas. Only a tiny nautical fridge under a fold-out ledge on the wall opposite, a copy of *The Joy of Cooking* propped open to a page she doesn't recognise, and a chopping block on which are laid out two pale and skinless carcasses, the size and shape of miniature rabbits.

"Where do you cook?" she asks.

Without a word, he lifts his face and raises his palms to the ceiling. There, slung up by ropes and pulleys, are a toaster oven, a hot plate, a cello, a music stand, and a wooden chair. He reaches for a winch and winds down the toaster oven, which makes a neat four-point landing on the ledge.

"See?" he says. "My kitchen!"

And then he picks up one tiny carcass and plunges the needle through its flesh, in and out, in and out.

"Are we having rabbit?" she asks.

He smiles. "You can keep a secret?"

"Yes," she says, wondering whether there are laws against killing baby rabbits, and how she could be implicated were she to eat one.

"Sqvuirrel," he says softly.

"What?"

"Zey fer eating my persimmons, so I shot zem. But ze landlord, he vould be werry werry mad if he found out. He doesn't comprehend ze vay ze ozer half lives."

———

A FEW WEEKS LATER, dropping off a box of old clothes at the symphony's secondhand shop, she notices a man trying on a pale yellow suit with bell-bottom trousers that stop above the ankles. "Brioni," he announces to her. "Imagine my luck! A thirty-eight long just died and went to heaven. What do you think?"

She thinks that he has lovely hands, cold eyes, a lovely Irish brogue. At the cafe next door, he tells her that he is writing his sixth novel, none of them published. The *cunths* in New York, he says, won't consider anything from California. They're into McInerney and Brent Ellis someone. If Dostoevsky were living now, he'd be selling shoes in Macy's. Forget about writing anything in the past tense. Forget about *story.*

When he gets to know her better, he calls her names, too. "Hello, *cunth,*" he says, or, if he's feeling particularly affectionate, "Hello, you old *cunth.*" His two-roomed apartment is a jumble of books and papers and clothes and bills. Dust and hair and the flimsy skeletons of insects waft here and there around the floor and furniture. Spiders have taken over the corners of everything. Mushrooms grow through cracks in the bathroom floor.

And yet, he will dine off nothing but china, which he also buys at the secondhand store. He will tolerate no stainless steel. He sends her a Valentine's Day card with bows and cherubs. And flowers for every occasion. Holidays make him sentimental. He counts up the months that they have known each other, takes her out for anniversary dinners. She wonders how he can afford such dinners. His means of support are almost invisible. The *cunths* at the IRS, he has told her, have bled him dry. They have no honor, no decency, no class.

Class, she discovers, is an obsession with him. So is being taken seriously as a suitor. When she comes over, he sweeps the dust under the furniture, puts out a fresh cake of soap, stashes the garbage in the refrigerator to keep the mice away. Some day, he assures her, polishing a wine glass, his ship will come in. She should stick with him, baby, he says, and she'll be farting through silk.

But she doesn't stick. She uses her accumulated mileage to go to Turkey, to Cairo, to Bombay. Far from home she finds that the curse is wearing off. She is tired of tour guides who write her rotten poetry in broken English. Of camel drivers with rotten teeth. Of men with strange smells, no money, and an eye out for a green card. She's running out of money herself. And she is surprised to find herself missing her Irishman. She phones him from Paris to say she is coming back. And buys a black lace garter belt and push-up bra as a joke for the occasion.

At JFK, she runs into an old friend, who has just married a banker and is writing a book on inner sex. Marriage, her friend confides over a drink, allows her to write full-time. It makes her family happy too, and her friends. And, even if the banker won't come to bed without flossing, or putting shoe trees into his shoes—even if he isn't someone to keep in mind when buying one's lingerie— still, he's just a man with a few bad habits. Quite acceptable, once you get over the death of the heart.

The Mirror

I CAME INTO THAT HOUSE OF SICKNESS JUST AFTER the Great War, as a girl of seventeen. They were there waiting for me, father and daughter, like a pair of birds, with their long noses and their great black eyes. The girl was a slip of a thing, no more than twelve, but she spoke up for the father in a loud, deep voice. Can you do this, Agnes? Have you ever done that? And the old man sat in his armchair with his watch chain and his penny spectacles, his pipe in his mouth and the little black moustache. Sometimes he said something to the girl in their own language, and then she would start up again. Agnes, do you know how to—

The wife was dying in the front parlor. They had moved a bed in there for her, and they kept the curtains drawn. In the lamplight, she looked a bit like a Red Indian, everything wide about her—eyes, mouth, nostrils, cheekbones. Even the hair was parted in the middle and pulled back into a plait.

From the start, she couldn't stand the sight of me. She would ring her little bell, and then, if I came in, give out one of her coughs, drawing the lips back from the raw gums to spit. And if that didn't do the trick, she growled and clawed her hands. So I had to call the native girl to go in and put her on the pot or whatever it was she wanted this time. I didn't mind. I hadn't come all this way to empty potties. They'd hired me as a housekeeper, and if the old woman was going to claw and spit every time I entered the room, well, soon she would be dead and I'd still be a housekeeper.

They gave me a little room on the third floor, very hot in the hot season, but it had a basin in it, and a lovely view of the racecourse. Every Saturday afternoon, I would watch the races from that window, the natives swarming in through their entrance, and the rickshaws, and then the Europeans in their hats, with their motorcars and drivers waiting. After a while, I even knew which horse was coming in, although I could only see the far stretch. But I never went down myself, even though Saturday was my day off, and I never laid a bet.

I kept my money in a purse around my neck, day and night. I didn't trust the natives, and I didn't trust the old man I worked for. Every week, he counted out the shillings into my palm, and one before the last he would always look up into my face with a smile to see if I knew he had stopped too soon. The daughter told me it was a little game he played. But I never saw him play it on the natives. There were two of them, male and female, and they lived in a corrugated iron shack in the garden. My job was to tell them what to do, and to see they didn't mix up dishes for fish and dishes for meat, which they did all the time regardless.

It was the daughter who had recited the rules of the kitchen for me, delivering the whole palaver in that voice of hers, oh Lord! And once, when there was butter left on the table and the meat was being carved, it was she who called me in and held out the butter dish as if it had bitten her on the nose. And the old man, with his serviette tucked into his collar, set down the carving knife and put a hand on her arm, and said, Sarah. So Sarah shut up.

There were other children, too, but they were grown up and married. Some of the grandchildren were older than this Sarah, older than me too. One of the grandsons fancied me. He was about my age, taller than the rest, and he had blue eyes and a lovely smile. But I hadn't come all the way out to South Africa to give pleasure to a Jewboy, even a charmer. I meant to make a marriage of my own, with a house and a servant, too.

And then, one day, the old man sent up a mirror for my room, and I stood it across one corner. It was tall and oval, and fixed to a frame so that I could change the angle of it by a screw on either side. And for the first time ever I could look at myself all at once, and there I was, tall and beautiful, and there I took to standing on a Saturday afternoon, naked in the heat, shameless before myself and the Lord.

Perhaps the old man knew. When I came into the room now, he would look up from his newspaper and smile at me if Sarah wasn't there. And, under his gaze, it was as if we were switched around, he and I, and he were the mirror somehow, and I were he looking at myself and knowing what there was to see, the arms and the legs, the breasts and the thighs, the hair between them. And in this way I became a hopeless wanton through the old man's eyes, in love with myself and the look of myself. I couldn't help it. I smiled back.

And then, one Saturday afternoon, he knocked at my door and I opened it, and in he came as if we had it all arranged, and he went straight over to the mirror and looked at me through it. I looked, too, a head taller than he was, bigger in bone, and not one bit ashamed to be naked.

The first thing he did was to examine the purse around my neck, which I always wore, even in front of the mirror. He fingered it and smiled, and looked up into my face. I thought he might try to open it and start up one of his games, but he didn't. He left it where it was and put his hands on my waist, ran them up to my breasts and put his face into the middle of them. And then he took them one at a time, and used his lips and his tongue and the edge of his teeth, and all this silently except for the jangle of my purse and the roar of the races outside. And, somehow, he unbuttoned himself and had his clothes off and folded on the chair without ever letting me go. And we were in and out of the mirror until he edged me to the bed and there we were, in the heat, under the sloping ceiling, the old man and me, me and me, and I never once thought of saying I wasn't that sort of girl. And when he had gone and I found a pound note on the table, I didn't think so then, either. Money was what there was between us. I was hired as a housekeeper. And he had given me my mirror.

She found out about it, of course, the old cow downstairs. I heard her coughing out her curses at him, whining and weeping. But he didn't say much. And when Sarah came to find me in the kitchen parlor and announced in that voice of hers that I was never to go into her mother's room again, who did she think she was punishing?

Still, I felt sorry for Sarah, ugly little thing, flat in the chest, with the thin arms and the yellow skin, and a little moustache on the upper lip. I would have told her how to bleach it, but she wouldn't look at me now. Nor would she look at her father. She sat at the table with her eyes fiercely on the food, saying nothing at all. It was only to her mother that she would speak willingly, rushing into the front parlor when she came home from school, performing her recitations there, as if the old woman could understand a word of them.

For me, the house was separated in another way—up there, where it was airy and he came to kneel before me in silence, and down here the dark sickness, the smells of their food and the sounds of their language, the natives mooching around underfoot.

And meanwhile, my money mounted up. The old man kept to the habit of leaving some for me every time. Not always a pound, but never less than two and sixpence. After a while, there was far too much to fit into the purse, so I hid the notes in a place I had found between the mirror and the wooden backing of it, and the larger coins inside the stuffing of my pillow. And, one Wednesday, when I had the afternoon off, I took it out of the hiding places and went down to the Building Society and put it in there. But still, I wore my purse around my neck, and he loved to notice it there, and to smile as he began to unbutton.

His teeth were brown from the pipe, with jagged edges to them, and his legs and arms were thin and yellow like Sarah's, with black hair curling. But I didn't have to ask myself what it was about his oldness and his ugliness that I waited for so impatiently at my mirror. The younger men, the beautiful young men I saw going to the races, or on my way into town, or even the sons and the grandsons of the household, who were always looking at me now, but not in the same playful way—they would bend me to themselves, these young men, require a certain sort of looking back at them, and a laughing into the future. Oh, no.

In the evenings, I brought the old man his sherry on a tray. He drank a lot for a Jew—two or three sherries, and wine, too, when he felt like it. And then once he looked up at me as I put down the tray, and there I was in that moment wondering how I could bear to wait until Saturday, and somehow he knew this because that night he came up the back stairs after Sarah was quiet in her room, and in the candlelight it was even better, the curves and the colours, my foot in his hand, pink in the candlelight as he put it to his cheek, and then held it there as he slid his other hand along the inside of the thigh. And I have never felt so strongly the power of being alive.

And then one Saturday afternoon, I was at the mirror waiting, and the door opened and it was Sarah to say they had called in the doctor, her mother was dying. Except that she didn't get it out because of the sight of me there, naked, with my purse around my neck. And I just smiled at her, because this was my room and she had no business coming in without knocking, and also I liked the look on her face as she gazed at me. And then, as I sauntered to the wardrobe for something to cover myself with, she said, I knocked, but you didn't hear, and she said it so politely for once, and in a normal voice, that I turned and I saw that she was crying, the eyes wide open and staring while the tears found a course around the nose and into the mouth. And she looked so frail, gaping there like a little bird, and she would be so lost now that the cursing old bitch was actually dying, that I went to her, naked as I was, and put my arms around her, and she didn't jump back, but buried her face between my breasts as her father did, and held me around the waist, snorted and wept against me for a while.

The races are on, I said, to calm her down, and Shall I dress and come downstairs? But she just held on tighter, and I saw that she was looking at us in the mirror, and there we were, a strange pair hugged together when he arrived in the doorway behind us, and, even so, we didn't turn, but stood there, all three of us staring at each other until he said something to her in their language and she sort of melted on the spot, folded down onto the floor in front of me, her hands around my ankles, weeping again. And of course I knew it had happened, the old woman was dead, and that it would change everything, had changed things already. There he stood in my mirror, a tired and ugly old man, muttering something to his youngest daughter. She would take over now, this strange bird at my feet. It was the way it would be, that I knew. And I must get dressed and find my way in the world.

Twilight

COMING TO AN ISLAND LIKE THIS WAS ALICE'S idea. "We should spend our old age together," she said, "you and me and Eva and who else?" I had several suggestions. And soon there was a whole network of us talking across the phone lines of America—my friends, their friends, like a tree full of birds. We'd buy a place somewhere without winter, we said, and we'd each live in a separate house, and write our novels, because who isn't writing a novel these days? And the men would come and visit, but they'd go away again, ha ha, the children as well.

I joined in. But the idea never really appealed. Living among women seems like a dangerous thing to do. Sooner or later, we'd be getting on one another's nerves. Eva's laugh, for instance, like a strangling chicken, which is what I'd find myself saying to Alice. Don't say anything, but—

Anyway, the life would be barren without men. And with men we'd be back where we started, talking to each other on the phone when the men were out of earshot. In all the talk, we never admitted we were one way with each other and another with our men. But that's how we are, every one of us.

And now here I am without them, without my man either. He was becoming a shadow, robe and slippers in the spare room closet, and the TV remote next to his chair. My chair. One day, I walked in as he was watching the news, and decided to sell both chairs, and the couch that went with them. After that, it was easy—piano, clocks, pictures, the house itself. It was a kind of intoxication, selling my life like that, and all the friends watching, holding their breath as I jumped.

"Perhaps," says Dr. Weimann, "it takes a shock to shake one free of one's fears?"

He is guessing, but he is wrong. The shock only came the day I arrived on this island. That night, and every night since, I've been shaken out of sleep by the old questions coming through to the surface. What will become of me? Who will I find to love?

Weimann lives in the annex at the back of the hotel. He has two rooms there, one of which is his office. Every morning, we go down to the water together. He swims straight out, stroke after stroke, right up to the reef, and then back again. I float just beyond waves, and even then, I look down to see what might be swimming below me.

"The sharks have quite enough to eat without considering you," he says. But still, I don't venture any farther.

Every evening at six, he comes down to the bar, which is really an old verandah, glassed in. The new verandah has been built around it like a fan, and doubles as the dining room. The whole hotel is built like that, rooms beyond rooms. It must once have been a house, plain and modest. The guest rooms themselves are plain and modest. They are spread along the front road like a barracks, with each door opening onto a narrow verandah.

Before I came here, I thought I'd find a cottage on the beach to live in, two rooms with tiled floors, perhaps, a hammock slung across one corner of the verandah. There would be morning trips to the local market, fish just caught, and island spices. And sometimes I might stroll over to the hotel for dinner. I might meet someone there or I might not. It wouldn't matter.

But now, three months have passed, and I'm still here in my little room at the end of the barracks. Except for the hotel beach, the coast on this side of the island is wild and steep and rough. Most of the locals live in squalid little shacks up in the hills. There are no cottages to rent.

"Shall we dine together tonight?" Weimann says.

People stand around us, a few of the more affluent natives, a couple of expats and their wives, who run a yacht for hire. It sits out in the bay like a castle. No doubt Weimann has slept with one of the wives. I can see from the way she avoids catching his eye, and then listens as he asks me about dinner.

When I thought up this idyll, I might have considered dinners, and the long nights afterwards. All I had to do was remember Crete—or Mauritius, or Papeete—sitting at a table for one, my bottle of wine corked for tomorrow, waiters offering themselves with a wink. But I never remember loneliness. From a distance, it always seems like peace.

The first week here, I sat in the hotel dining room with a book, or I walked down to the Harbour Café and ordered curried chicken. I thought I might walk along the beach afterwards, have a swim, perhaps, or sit out on the verandah to watch the last of the sun. But who could have imagined the evenings here? Half an hour of twilight, and then the dark comes right in.

Dearest E——   This hotel must once have been very grand, with its foyer and ballroom and balustrades and nymphs around the pool. I love that pool, halfway down the cliff, cracked, green with algae, overgrown. I go down there in the afternoons, when the wind picks up on the beach. This afternoon, I saw a snake slither into the vines, brighter green than anything around it. I watched the vine, hoping it would come out again, and wind itself around my wrist or my ankle, and bite. This isn't morbid, it's languid. It's content with the present at last. Which is what I am.

Weimann's skin is hairless, even the backs of his hands. And the fingernails are strangely convex, strangely purple. When he makes love to me, I have to shut my eyes against him. I try not to hear the moans he makes. He is moaning for me, not for himself. They are moans of encouragement, sound effects. And they revolt me.

So why go through with it? Alice would be the first to ask this. "What's in it for you?" she'd say.

I've never been able to answer Alice's questions. She wouldn't understand the sight of an old woman with a basket at the market this morning. Even as a young girl, I saw that old woman everywhere before me. She stood beside every man who raised a glass to me across a restaurant, beside Weimann himself, sending the waiter over with his card.

Eva would be easier. She'd say, "It makes one feel alive." And I'd be grateful for that. Eva is too beautiful to survive among women without such generosity. And anyway, she loves a daring act, she who is still one foot in and one foot out of marriage. Not that sleeping with a man like Weimann is daring, but that the trip itself delights her. She counts on me for daring.

Dearest E—   The boatman came from the mainland about twenty years ago, they tell me, using his hands to say that he wanted work. To me, his hands are his beauty—large-boned, lovelier

than a face. I watch them smoothing and smooth-
ing the satin edge of the blanket, as if he's finding
the words to say he has to leave me, leave the is-
land for good. He could play that part, Odysseus
the Wanderer. Without speech, he could play any
part I give him. His voice would be buoyant and
lyrical, like all the others on this island. Weimann
says it's unusual, being able to hear but not to
speak. He seems to pose this as a question, lean-
ing across the bar. "These people are clever with
words," he says, "and also without them." He
thinks I'll tire of the mute and come over to him.
But I have a dull time with words when I talk to
Weimann. I need to go looking for them, and,
when I do, they hide.

At dinner, Weimann does the ordering, but he makes
sure that the waiter puts the orders onto our separate ac-
counts. Even if he did pay for me, would this tiny act of
gallantry have me walking to his room with a lighter
heart? I don't think so. It would take some level of deceit
to pull me along that corridor, quick and sharp, like that
woman at the bar. I have been that woman, I know the appeal of rooms darkened in the afternoon, a man to leave
behind and another to go back to.

"Weimann," I say, "I find your moaning in bed
revolting."

He arches an eyebrow, continues shelling his prawns with his knife and fork, laying the shells neatly around the edge of the plate.

"What is appealing in a man is real desire," I say.

He looks up.

"Animal desire."

"And in a woman too," he says.

Alice was right. She was the one who came up with the quote I pinned above my desk: "The less you invest emotionally, the more you stand to lose."

I turn to look out at the last of the light over the sea. Down on the beach, a family is pulling in their catch. The father stands in the surf, the mother at the water's edge with a boy on either side.

"They seem happy," I say to Weimann. What I mean is that everything from which I've constructed a life seems like the baggage of nomads. Men, children, house, work. And yet, had I started out here, like those boys in the water, I'd have gone north as soon as I could. As they will too.

"You feel at home with this sort of happiness?" Weimann asks. He knows the answer, the old Nazi. Leave home long enough, and you find it again only in moments.

The dining room has the slightly sickish smell of seafood and sweet island fruits. Except for us and a Brazilian couple on honeymoon, the hotel is empty. Only the bar seems to keep it alive.

The main port is on the other side of the island. Cruise ships stop there, and there are shops and nightclubs and petty criminals. You have to take a boat to reach this town, or drive for eight hours over rough mountain roads. I chose it for this reason. I wanted to replenish, I said. Only Alice rolled her eyes. "'Languish' is more like it," she said. And even then I knew I should have chosen the port, and stayed in the grand hotel, and gone down to the shops in the afternoons.

But if I were to pack up now, and take the boat back around, I'd fly out for good. And if I flew out, where would I go, unreplenished? These are the questions I ask myself every morning after a night with Weimann.

Eva—   Weimann knows that the boatman comes up to my room by the back stairs. Everyone here knows, I suppose. There was never a question of his coming in through the front door, wiping his feet on the mat, smoothing down his hair. He arrives like a cat, like a leopard. I hardly hear the door handle, and then there he is, smelling of a day in the boat. He's older than I thought, probably forty-five or so, the body thick with muscle. Unless he's taking the boat out, he never hangs around the dock. There must be a woman in the hills, children too, probably. The delightful thing is, he's not interested in leaving the island. That's not what he's after.

Tonight, Weimann doesn't undress, nor does he invite me to take my own clothes off. He sits in his armchair, smoking, and I am grateful for this. His room gives nothing away. Double bed, wardrobe, two armchairs, stereo, TV, VCR. Only his medical instruments seem specific to him. Clean, spare, misshapen to a purpose. When he removed the sea urchin spine from my foot, his face lost all its mockery, its boredom, its lust.

"I have a surprise," he says. He gets up to pour us each a whiskey, stands waiting as I drink mine down like medicine, refills the glass. Suddenly I suspect he's been reading my e-mail, that he has the boatman hidden somewhere. That the boatman is to be my punishment. I begin to stand, but no, he's slipping a cassette into the VCR, switching off the lamps, coming back to his chair with the remote.

The show starts with a woman, face down on a lawn, naked. At first, she looks dead, but really she's sunbathing, she's sleeping. Weimann has the sound turned off. All I can hear is the buzz of the TV, the surf outside.

A Great Dane comes up to her and starts licking her buttocks, licking and licking until she wakes up. She turns, annoyed, a hopeless actress. But then she opens her legs a little, and the licking continues. She raises herself in the air, rises on all fours, and he mounts her, he's trying to find the way in, ducking and thrusting the way dogs do. The camera is underneath them now, you can see the pinkness of the dog and of her too.

Weimann cannot know how I go about making his smooth, womanish skin desirable, the dead weight of his flesh on top of me. And yet here it is, this dog ducking and thrusting, this baboon, this donkey, this beast of desire. Helpless with it, blind, deaf, mute.

But now I have seen the dog, and it is as sad as a circus lion. When I saw the hotel for the first time, when the boatman carried in my suitcases, and stared at me in that way of his until I gave him a tip—when I stood at the front desk, wondering what I would do in the heat of the afternoon, and all the afternoons that lay ahead—I lost the peace of those two rooms with tiled floors, and the hammock, and the little desk in one corner with a view out over the water, even of the water itself, the way it has always seemed to stretch one life into another.

"Weimann," I say, standing up, "I'm not your woman for this."

Alicia Preciosa—   Would you remind me what was so boring about Peter? He made me laugh, didn't he? I need you on this, my dear, don't let me down. And don't worry about the boatman. It was safe. And it's over.

The day after the Great Dane, a woman arrives at the hotel. She is thick and grey and spectacled, and her clothes are too heavy for the climate—socks and lace-up shoes, slacks, a jacket. I watch the boatman stand behind her, waiting for his tip. But there's an argument with the manager. She won't abandon her passport, not even overnight.

The manager looks at me for help.

And so I step up and tell her that it's all right, it's the law, she'll get her passport back tomorrow. That I was worried too, but it was all right.

She hands it over then, and turns to me, and says, "I don't know why I came here."

"Tip the boatman," I whisper.

"What? Ah! Yes! Here—"

"Would you like to come down to the beach this afternoon?" I say.

"Ah. Well. I work in the afternoons. See you later, then?"

But I don't see her again for six days. Even though it is impossible to disappear in this place, she has done it. She is not in the dining room in the evenings, nor is she at the Harbour Café, nor on the beach. At one point I think Weimann must have her roped to his bed. At least this is what I write to Eva. The arrival and disappearance of this woman has cheered me up, somehow. Why don't we all meet at the port in April? I suggest to Eva. I'll book us into the hotel there. It'll be like a trial run.

By the time I see the new woman walking along the front one afternoon, I've found out from the manager that she has her meals sent to her room, and that she moved to the annex because of the noise along the front. "Always, always," he says, making typing motions with his fingers.

I hurry to catch up to her. She is storming along in a pair of native sandals and a lurid muslin beach dress she must have bought at the market. "Hello!" I say.

She stops dead. "Oh! You! Hi!" She holds out a hand. "Letty," she says. "Hi."

She's wearing a baseball cap with green sequins on it, and there's a little moustache, wide nostrils, sallow skin.

"Want something cold to drink?" I walk ahead to the cold drink stand before she can answer. "Let's go out onto the jetty."

But she stops at the bottom of the steps, staring into the surf. "I can't swim," she says.

"You won't have to. You'll be safe. Come on."

And she does. She climbs the steps and walks close behind, obedient, like a child. I find a place for us to sit, and she takes the Fanta, drinks it greedily. The sun is blinding on the water. No one except the boatman is out, and even he is trawling about lazily in the dinghy.

"What do you write, Letty?"

"Gothic. Like my name. Letitia. Mysteries mostly. You?"

"Me?"

"Oh. I saw you with the laptop, and I thought, oh, you know, you must be at it too, and I can't talk about it, 'specially when I'm in the middle. Any time, really."

"I've been writing e-mail," I say. "I plug it in at the office."

"Oh. E-mail. Can't cope with any of that."

I'd planned the e-mail even before I came here. Calypso on her island. Or Scylla and Charybdis, both as men. Or Persephone. Or something. Every day I print them out, thinking that sooner or later I'll be ready, I'll want to start. Every night, a story seems possible, and every morning I go down to the beach for a swim. And then, when I come back, the words are nothing, they are less than nothing. They cheat and they lie. And now, sitting here with Letty, I don't want anything to do with them anymore.

"Met our Goebbels yet?" I ask.

She stares at me.

"The doctor. Weimann."

She throws her head back in a roaring laugh. "Oh! Dr. Weimann!" She swings her legs over the water, peers to one side, then the other, as if she's having a conversation with herself. "Keep a secret? I'm putting him into the novel. Well, not him so much as that glove collection."

"*Glove* collection?" I am back at school now, laughter at the far end of the hockey field that stops when I walk up. "What sort of gloves?" I say.

"Haven't you *seen*? *Dozens* of them, all wrapped in blue tissue! Beautiful ones with fur, and lace ones, and lots of long kid gloves. Oh, and a tiny pair of children's gloves with the fingertips cut off. And a gauntlet with the blood marks still on it. And one with no thumb on one hand. Wouldn't you say Goering? Rather than Goebbels?" Another roar.

Weimann and I still dine together, although I don't go back to his room any more, and he's never on the beach when I am. When I ask him about the new woman, he shrugs. "Perhaps she's at home with her own happiness?" he says.

I throw the straw into the water and watch it float in, up, over. "What about the boatman?" I say.

"Huh?"

"For the novel. The mute. Out there in the dinghy. He carried your bags up?"

She seems to consider this for a moment, sucking in the last of her Fanta. "Na. No blacks, no Jews, no Germans. I had to make the doctor Danish, a Danish count."

"Has he shown you his porn?"

"Pornography? Really? Oh, goody!"

"Letty," I say, "wouldn't you like to come to the dining room tonight?"

She cocks her head. "Would I not, no? Or would I not, yes? Yes, I think I would, yes. Why not? I can take a little break, now."

THAT EVENING, SHE arrives at the bar in a dirndl with a frilly white blouse underneath. She has parted her hair in the middle and tied it into a ponytail. People turn to watch her, to watch us as I lead her out to the dining room. I have chosen a table next to the window, far from Weimann's. When the waiter comes to take our orders, I tell him to put them both onto my account. I glance quickly at Weimann, who is still at the bar. The yacht people have brought in some tourists and they are all drinking together. I order a bottle of claret, and, when it arrives, send a glass over to him.

She tells me that she came here because she was stuck, and she had read an article—warm places where you won't find tourists. "Everything in it was wrong," she says, "except about the tourists. But so what, hey? Here I am. Unstuck." She lifts her glass and slugs back the wine.

I don't tell her that it was I who wrote that article, wrote it without even coming here. That I often did that, and no one seemed to know the difference.

"Let's go swimming after dinner," I say. "I'll teach you." A full moon hangs low over the water. The night is bright with it, the water is brilliant.

But she shakes her head.

"We can stay in the shallows."

"No, it's hopeless. It's like horses. I'm terrified of them too, doesn't matter how many times I try. I write about them, but I can't go near them."

"In my e-mails, I write about an affair I'm not having," I say. "I write about a hotel I'm not staying at too.

And about happiness I'm not feeling. It's easier than the other way around."

"You see," she says, "I knew we'd be talking about it sooner or later."

THERE ARE NO WAVES, just swells, the way I love it. And the water is warm, black as ink under the moon, perfect. With her on the beach to watch, I plunge straight in, swim out without stopping. With her shouting "Careful!", I swim farther than I've ever been before. I dive under and stay there for a while. When I come up, she is at the water's edge, waving both arms. I wave back. I start to sing. The water makes me happy, it has always made me happy. "That's because you're a water sign," Alice would say, she holds with that sort of thing.

But this is more than just the water. An old happiness is lifting my heart and voice and spirit all at once, all with the lovely water, with the lovely hymn I begin to sing. "Praise my soul the King of Heaven, To His feet thy tribute bring." I am singing for a future still to be had, and glorious things that will happen, places to go, and, oh, people to come back to.

I am out near the reef now, I can hear the water breaking there. And something is swimming with me, it brushes against my arm, light, almost liquid, a jellyfish perhaps, a ripple in the water. I stop singing and watch the water, but it is full of shapes, silver and black, a few ripples beginning to crest with the tide coming in. Whatever it is—even finned, even toothed—it feels like a lover. And if it came and took me down with it, down and down right to the bottom, that would be perfect too. I would be happy.

But then it is gone, and the tide is carrying me in, easy. There is Letty, still waving, I'd forgotten her for a moment. I swim in, swell after swell. And that's when I see Weimann on the sand with her, waving too. Both of them are still in their shoes. Standing side by side, they look like one of those odd German couples who take bus tours around Europe, and sleep in cubbyholes under the bus, and live out of a backpack.

As I come out of the water, she runs at me, flaps her arms. She wants to embrace me, perhaps, but I'm wet.

"Did you not notice that no one has been swimming all day?" Weimann says. His voice is shrill, insistent. It has lost its slippery edge, the dip and rise over a question.

I prance a little before him, before her too, go off to find my towel so that they have to follow.

"Are you not aware of the manta ray out there?" he demands. "Are you quite mad?" He considers my body as if he's never seen it, his eyes very pale in the light. "Your boatman has been trying to spear it all day."

"*My* boatman?"

"Oh," says Letty. "I told him. You know. Your idea for the novel."

Alice of my heart—   *Goebbels collects* gloves!
*He invited me to see them this afternoon. And so
off I went, thinking, "Etchings," but no, my dear,
nothing of the sort. His room is separate from the
hotel, right at the back, and Gothic has a room
there too. Coming down the passage, I heard a sort
of moaning, man or woman, hard to tell which,
and I stopped, but just then his door opened, and
Gothic tripped out, all dainty on her size 10s,
tripped down to her door and slipped in.*

They are coming in April, Alice and Eva and a few of
the others too. We will meet at the port, and stay in the big
hotel. Until then, I'll stay on here, it's not long. And afterwards, we'll all go back together. Already, they're looking out for a condominium for me, one bedroom, with
a gardening service included, and a lovely view of the
water. There'll be lunches just for us, with asparagus and
salmon and laughing. And, on the weekends, we'll be with
our men, as usual. Men out on the patio with drinks in the
long summer evenings. Men watching us laugh. Watching
for danger.

Selina Comes to
the City

THERE WAS NO QUESTION OF A SEND-OFF. A GROUP at the roadside with her, waiting for the bus to come. She had a pass. Her child was weaned. And she was sixteen. Time to go to the city.

Selina Nsome. Mission station girl. Daughter of the minister's helper. A Methodist mission. A Methodist God. "Oh God Almighty, who took my sister to His bosom, do not take her child from me. Do not take my child either," she sang, sitting on her box of clothes, waiting for the bus to come.

February. The summer sun sucked water from the rivers, from the sea, and held it in a heavy haze over the fields of cane and burnt sienna earth. Selina wore her mother's dress, too small already for her breasts and stomach, but good for finding work. A mission dress, with long sleeves. And shoes with laces. Stockings. A black straw hat tied under the chin.

A car flew by, coating her with red dust. She reached into her pocket and unfolded again the address of her cousin's cousin in the city, stared at the uneven printing, and put it back.

"My sister is dead," she hummed, "my twin, my Emma, my light-skinned, bad-luck sister. Oh Lord Almighty, you have punish me already for my sister's light skin. Punish the father of her child. Punish that father for his snake's tongue. Punish him for his snake's voice. Punish him for my legs that opened for him when she was dead. Make his manhood dry up. Let the white man take away his pass."

Mission girls, barefoot, pious. One dark, one light. One dead. Ai! Selina hung her head and wept. For Emma. For herself. For the blame she had to bear from her father for nothing she could do. He was the minister's helper. He knew that God giveth and God taketh away. He knew we are all God's children, light skin, dark skin. But it was *she* he called child of the devil. It was *she* he had beaten with a stick when there was to be another child. Emma he had forgiven. The firstborn. The clever one. The teacher for his mission school.

And now to turn away from Walter, already walking ten months from his birth, ten months from his mother's death, and clever like his mother. And naughty like his mother. Dark-skinned and fat like Selina. And to love so much her own Abigail, the color of milky mabella. A mix-up. Ai!

The bus curled down from the foothills, marking its course with a cloud of red dust. Selina watched it approach. She picked up her box and stood at the edge of the road. She waved. The bus slowed down and stopped.

"Chêcha!" the driver said.

She pushed her box ahead of her up the steps and then climbed on herself. The bus smelled of sweat and the smoke of homemade cigarettes. Some men at the back shouted comments about her hips. They invited her to sit with them. She pulled her box onto an empty bench and sat beside it, her skin and clothes wet with the wait and the effort. She stared out of the window at the poles flying past, the cane, the kraals and hills and trees she knew. Walter and Abigail. Time was nothing. Sadness was nothing. The city was nothing. Men were nothing.

"YOU'RE NOT afraid of work?"

"I'm not afraid of work, Madam."

"Any references?"

"No references, Madam."

"You've never worked before?"

"No, Madam."

They stood at the kitchen door with the smells of rubbish from the bins outside, and the dogs whining to be let out. Selina trusted this white woman. She was small and ugly and she never smiled. But she had a space between her front teeth. That meant truth and faithfulness. She had a baby in her stomach. Her voice was deep and polite, like a man's. And the cook had told her that she kept out of the kitchen.

"The job is for a nanny. Have you ever looked after children?"

Selina dropped her eyes to the floor. "Yes, Madam."

"Whose?"

"I'm got a baby, Madam. My sister she died, I'm got her baby too."

"Good heavens! How old are these children?"

"Not yet one year, Madam."

"I see." The white woman looked doubtful.

"The children they stay with their grandmother," Selina said quickly. "They stay at the Mission Station."

The white woman nodded. She looked at Selina for a long time, at her face, her hands, the dress she wore. "Well, Selina," she said at last. "I'll tell you that I like you. You seem to be a nice sort of girl. Clean. Willing. And honest. I hope I'm not wrong."

"You not wrong, Madam."

"But you're *young*. And there will be *lots* of work. My son is eight years old. My daughter is seven. And the new baby is coming in five months. The Master and I are often gone."

"Yes, Madam. I can work." Why two and then one, Selina wondered? She stared at the ground, waiting and hoping.

"When can you start?"

"Today, Madam."

"Well then fetch your things. I'll tell Agnes, the housekeeper, to have your room prepared. —Oh, and Selina, we're going to have to do something about your body odour."

"Yes, Madam." What was the white woman talking about? She would have to ask her cousin's cousin.

"I'll provide you with Mum to start with and then you must buy your own. You must use it *every* day. Agnes will give you soap. And uniforms."

"Thank you, Madam."

The cousin's cousin told her she was lucky. A room and a bed to herself. New uniforms. Boys' meat every night. But still it was lonely to sleep in a room all alone. No roosters in the morning. No fire smell. No goats. No mission bell. No singing. "Rock of Ages," she hummed to herself. But her humming couldn't fill up her head. Her sadness stopped her wanting the meat. She gave hers to the others. At night she cried softly into her pillow and made it wet. Where was the lucky? She wanted Walter. She wanted Abigail. She wanted Emma. But Emma was dead.

ONLY THE CHILDREN made her happy. Even the bad one, the jealous girl. Even when they used bad words and pulled off her cap and hid it away from her. They made her laugh, like brothers and sisters.

"Selina, you mustn't allow those children to be rude to you."

"They not rude, Madam."

She never gave the children away. And they, in return, did not turn their play into oppression. On her days off she visited her cousin's cousin. Or her cousin's cousin came to her. When she took the children to the park on Saturday afternoons she met other nannies. They sat in the shade and talked while the children climbed and ran and fought. She stood with the nannies who pushed small children on swings and listened to what they had to say about life in the city.

Selina learned a lot. She learned to knit and to crochet. On Thursday afternoons now she would put on her dress and lace-up shoes and walk down through the race course to town. The other nannies had told her that wools and cottons were cheap in Indian town. And so she went there. They had warned her that Indians cheat. So she shook her head at the prices they gave her. Until they stopped following her out of the shop. Then she paid the last price they'd asked. Her new friends told her how to sell her doilies and tea cosies to Billinghams. And how to buy a postal order so that no one could steal her money when she sent it home. They warned her not to argue with a Madam. To stay silent even in anger. They told her how to make sure she didn't get a baby. But she shook her head at this. "Hayi!" she said. And then they laughed. Because she was beautiful. And the houseboys and garden-boys always shouted to her as she passed.

One day she learned how to get a whole weekend off to go home. You must write a letter and tell them to send a telegram back, they said. "Mother sick come home." Then you must take it to the Madam and look sad. She won't believe you but she will let you go. And you must always come back on time, they warned. Selina wrote the letter.

"Madam," she said, standing at the lounge door, dropping her chin, staring at the floor.

"What is it, Selina?"

"Madam, a telegram—" She held out the envelope.

The Madam rolled her eyes and shook her head. "Don't tell me, I know already. Your aunty is sick and you have to go home. That it?"

"My mother, Madam."

The Madam sighed. It was okay. *"When?"* she demanded.

But Selina just stared at the ground as instructed.

"Well, I suppose I have no choice." She sighed again. "Although you *could* have picked a better moment. Three weeks until this baby arrives. P.G."

"Yes, Madam."

"All right, Selina. Leave on Friday after dinner. And be back by Sunday night."

But Selina didn't move.

"What now?"

"Madam, Friday is first of the month. Many tsotsis on the buses." She had knitted clothes for the children, bought biscuits for them and packets of sweets. She had collected money in an envelope. She didn't want her treasures stolen, herself in the hospital with a knife in her ribs.

Another sigh. "Thursday evening then. And Selina, this had better *not* happen too often."

"No, Madam. Thank you, Madam."

THE BUS WAS crowded and hot. Selina stood for the first two hours. But then people got off. She saw her world again through the windows, the river in flood now with summer rains, cattle on the high ground, huddled among the wattles for shade. The bus passed the coolie store and then the dam. "Ai!" she called out. "Lapa."

It slowed and squeaked and stopped. Selina climbed out into the dust with her new cardboard suitcase. Someone waved at her from the well. She waved back. As she approached the mission a few of the kraal dogs came out and barked and wagged around her, sniffing the city in her clothes and on her skin.

She could hear singing in the church and from the children playing games with stones. She stopped and put down her suitcase. People had seen her now. Some of them called out. The children ran towards her hoping for sweets. Then she saw her mother come out of the hut wiping her mouth with her arm. She saw Walter, strutting now, behind her. And Abigail on her back. Her mother came to stand in front of her, swaying slightly on her feet. Her eyes were red. She smelled of Kaffirbeer.

Kneeling in the church, Selina clasped her hands together and shut her eyes. "Oh, Lord Almighty," she prayed, "you are the Father, I am the child. Sometimes, you give me good luck, thank you for that. If bad things happen, you know why. I try to understand. I read your book. Time is nothing. Sadness is nothing. The city is nothing. I am nothing."

THE DOCTOR HAD come already for the Madam. But the Madam didn't scream or even shout. Selina laughed. White women liked to shout at the wrong times.

It was Sunday. She had been sent into the garden with the children to wait, and sat with her knitting under the avocado pear tree. "Nearer, my God to thee," she warbled to herself.

The white nurse was up there for the baby. Do this, do that! Selina spat on the ground. What kind of nurse with no baby of her own? Old too, ugly too. Uglier than the Madam.

Someone shouted. And faintly, under the voices, there was the cry of a baby. Selina's breasts grew hard. Her womb tightened. She stood up to listen. A baby crying,

crying. There were tears in her own eyes. Her chest weeping, her womb mourning.

A window flew open. "A girl! Another girl!" But the children were in the tree shouting and didn't hear.

"Wê Andrew! Wê Margaret! Come down! You got a sister! Your mother she have a girl!"

FOR MORE THAN a year, while the white baby grew, Selina had no chance to go home. Every month she sent a letter and a postal order and, once, a snap that Andrew had taken of her with his new camera. But nothing came back. Then, one day, Agnes handed her another telegram. "You better watch out," she said.

COME HOME IMMEDIATELY. WALTER DEAD.

"Aiii!" Selina shrieked. She picked up the baby and ran to the kitchen. "Aiiii!" Not once did she doubt the truth of the message. Dead. Dead. Dead like his mother. The baby in her arms began to whimper.

"All *right*, Selina. All *right*, my girl. Calm *down*! I *do* believe you. You may go tonight. Right away if you wish." The Master watched her sniffing and snorting. "Come," he said. "I'll drive you to the bus stop."

"Thank you, Master."

"Do you need money for the funeral?"

For a cow, yes. Or at least a goat. Some beer. A box to bury him in. "Thank you, Master."

"What did he die of? Do you know?"

But she knew enough, even in her grief, not to answer this. T.B. or cholera and they wouldn't have her back. "Master, the child he always been sick."

WHEN SHE RETURNED, the Madam called the white doctor to the house to check her up. He looked everywhere—ears and mouth and front and back. Even between her legs. But he couldn't find her sick. It was a sickness in her heart that she suffered. She didn't sing anymore. She sat still, like a rock or a chair, and let the baby climb all over her.

One day, when the Madam and the Master were gone out, the baby pinched her breast. She jumped. It pinched again and laughed. She laughed. They were in the gazebo. No one could see. She picked up the baby, fat and laughing, held it in her arms like an infant. She kissed the baby's hair, kissed its mouth, held it tight against her. It laughed and laughed, pinched her again. Then she plunged her hand into her uniform and pulled out her round, plump breast. The baby poked at it with small fingers. She picked up the nipple and pushed it to the child's mouth. It looked up at her, not remembering what to do. "Mê! Mê!" she said, sucking in the air with her lips. "Mê!" The baby closed its mouth on her nipple and blew. It laughed at the noise. Then it took the breast in two hands and sucked. Sucked so that Selina's thighs weakened and her womb cried out. She clasped the baby to her and rocked back and forth, back and forth. "Ai, ai, ai," she crooned. "Ai, ai, ai."

THAT NIGHT, WHEN the next-door houseboy came to visit, she didn't chase him away. She opened her legs to him. And again the next night. And again. And again. She didn't remember what the other nannies had told her. She only waited for her work to be over, for the dark of her room and her dark night lover.

A few months later it had happened. No bleeding. The sickness. She went to her friends and asked what to do. They told her about the woman with the needle, and then about the doctor at the hospital who would fix you for good afterwards if you liked.

She went one night to the woman with the needle. Paid, suffered, bled. The next week she told the Madam she wanted that doctor to fix her. Her friends told her white women would pay.

"But Selina," this one said, "are you *certain* about this? Look how you love Elizabeth. Don't you want time to think it over?"

Selina shook her head. "Madam, I can pay you back every month."

"It's not the *money*, Selina! Of *course* I'll give you the money! It's just that I want you to be *sure* you understand what you're doing."

"I understand, Madam."

———

SO NOW THERE was only Abigail. And a box for her future. For her to be a teacher like Emma. Selina's friends told her about a bank, and the savings book where they wrote down the money so that no one could steal it away. On Thursday she walked to town with her chocolate box of notes and coins under her arm. She stood in the non-European line and waited.

"I have to count all *this?*" the white lady said.

"Yes, Madam. Please, Madam."

The woman counted. But Selina knew already how much it was.

"Madam, *four*teen," she said. "Not thirteen."

"*What?* You don't trust me, you monkey? Here, let's see you count it yourself."

Slowly Selina counted while the white lady sighed and rolled her eyes. Carefully she separated the coins into units, the notes into piles. "*Four*teen, Madam," she said.

"Ugh! Jeeslike!" the woman said. "One pound off and you'd think it's the end of the world!"

ONE SUNDAY, BEFORE Christmas, Selina's mother brought Abigail on the bus. They needed more money she said. A window for the house. Bricks.

"What house?" Selina asked.

"For the mission teacher. For Abigail. Your house."

Seventeen and sixpence in the box. Selina spilled it into her mother's lap. Her mother's hands shook as she spread out the change and tried to count. Her teeth were gone. Her clothes were dirty. She smelled sweet and sour with Kaffirbeer.

The old woman took the money and left the child with Selina. A quiet child, she sat on the floor of Selina's room. If Selina gave her a sponge or a comb or a flower, she stared into it, turned it over, and put it down again. A good child. Never cried. Not when Selina left her alone in the room. Not even when the food was late.

"Madam, my child she's here."

"Yes, I noticed that Selina."

Selina stared at the floor.

"It's a lovely baby, Selina, but who's looking after it?"

"I look after, Madam."

"What about when you're working?"

"The child she is a good child, Madam."

"How old is she?"

"Two years, Madam, and six months."

"And how long—you know she can't *stay* here, don't you?"

"Yes, Madam. —Madam, Christmas—"

"What?"

"Please Madam, give me Christmas. I take the baby back."

"No Selina. I'm *very* sorry. How on *earth* do you think we'll manage on our holiday without a nanny for Elizabeth?"

Selina hung her head. Some white women's questions needed no answers.

"You'll have to take the child back before we go." She sighed. "Next Saturday I suppose. You know, this is beginning to be a nuisance, Selina?"

"Yes, Madam. Sorry, Madam."

THE CHILDREN MET on the laundry lawn when the Madam was sleeping. Face to face they stood and stared at each other like dogs. Selina and Dora, the laundry girl, watched from the shade of the laundry room door. "Play! Play!" Selina whispered.

But Abigail looked down now, well taught to keep her eyes from the soul of another. The smaller one swaggered around the stranger, wearing only a wet nappy. Dora and Selina laughed softly at the wet nappy, at the monkey face and monkey look of her. Little white monkey, little white monkey. Black child with money locked up in a bank. Quiet black child with the time to learn. They clucked in pleasure like aunties.

Closer and closer the monkey came. She pushed the stranger and nearly fell backwards herself with the effort. But the stranger was firm and stout like her mother. She stood still and looked at the grass.

The women in the doorway laughed at the contest. "Oo-hoo! Ee-hee!"

At their laughing the monkey jumped on her wide-apart feet and grabbed at the stranger's arm. She bit down on the plump black hand with her new sharp teeth.

"Ai!" The black child ran, without tears, behind her mother's skirt. Hung on tight.

"Na! Na!" The monkey ran too, held up her arms to be picked up, danced from foot to foot and cried loudly, also without tears. She stared down over Selina's shoulder at the other. Bounced in Selina's arms to ungrasp the stranger from the skirt.

"Thula!" Selina whispered. "ukuThula!" She patted the monkey's nappy softly. "Thula! Thula!"

But behind now, into the skirt, tears came. And small low grunts. Rhythmical, breathy with a year-old cough.

"Thula!" Selina scolded over her shoulder.

The grunts only grew into sobs, low and insistent.

Selina reached behind her with one hand and hit, hard, the back of her own child's head.

"Aaaah!" the child wailed, high and low, the sound broken into two notes by the damp in her lungs.

And now the monkey too cried, real tears. She clung tight around Selina's neck and shrieked.

A window flew open half an hour before the end of sleep time. "*What* is going on out there? Selina? Dora? *Why* is Elizabeth crying so loudly?"

Selina moved out of the shade to be shouted at properly. But Abigail moved out with her, still clinging to her skirt. And Elizabeth, yoke between two mothers, opened her monkey mouth wide at her mother above and yelled in outrage.

"If *this* is what is going to *happen* every time you

bring that child here, Selina, I'm going to have to *forbid* it. Do you understand?"

"Yes, Madam. Sorry, Madam."

The children wailed high and low.

"Selina, *deal* with those children please. Give them a biscuit or something."

"Thank you, Madam."

The window slammed shut.

"uku *Thula!*" Selina shouted. She turned, Elizabeth still over her shoulder, and slapped Abigail on her fat wet cheek. Pulled her up roughly by the arm and dragged her, her legs just above the ground, back through the compound gate and into her room. Slammed the door shut. *"Thula!"* she shouted. "Inhlu*p*heko!"

NOTHING LOOKED NEW. No smoothed-out place for a new house, no bricks. Selina stopped on the koppie for a better view.

"Gogo! Gogo!" Abigail struggled down off her hip and ran.

The old woman staggered under the impact of the child in her arms. She sat down on a rock and let the child lay her head on her lap.

"Where is the house?" Selina asked.

The old woman giggled, clasped one hand over her mouth. "Over there!" She flung a ragged arm towards the station and the kraal.

"Gogo! Gogo!" Abigail said.

Things smelled funny this time. Goat excrement. Human excrement. Even the smokiness of the thatch. Even her mother—Kaffirbeer mixed now with body odour, with the stale smell of her old age.

"There is no house," Selina said.

The old woman shook her head.

"Mother, where is my seventeen and sixpence?"

"Ha! Ha!"

No house, no bricks, no window. The money gone on beer.

"Mother, what about my child?"

Abigail clung fast to the old woman, closing her eyes against Selina's claim.

Selina planted her hands on her hips. "No more money for a house!" she said.

"No money for food," the old woman croaked. "How will we feed your child?"

"Where is Father? I will give Father my money."

"He will give it to me." The old woman peeled her lips back from pink gums and cackled. "He will not talk to you. To him you are the child of the devil."

"Gogo!" Abigail cried. "Gogo!"

"Hee-hee! Hee-hee!" the old woman cackled. "Your father is silent. Your uncles are gone. Your sister is dead. Only me."

An old man came out of the church in threadbare black vestments. He stood for a moment in the sun, shaded his eyes with his hand.

The child ran to him.

He bent to pat her head. "Ai! Ai!" he said.

"Father!" Selina shouted.

He turned away from her with the child's hand in his. "The Lord's my shepherd, I'll not want," he sang in a deep rich baritone.

Selina picked up her suitcase and followed him. "Father! Talk to me! Mother buys drink with my money. What will happen to my child?"

"He makes me down to lie—" he sang.

Abigail laughed, danced next to him to the rhythm of his singing.

"I work hard for that money. I have a book from the bank. Maybe a Christmas bonsella too."

"In pastures green He leadeth me, the quiet waters by."

SELINA STOOD AT the swings now, pushing with the other nannies.

"Higher! Higher!"

They had told her how to send food home through the post. Not money anymore. They told her to pay the teachers straight. To buy the books herself. To ask the Madam for paper, pencils, crayons. Madams liked to be asked for these things.

"Selina! Higher!"

She must ask for old school uniforms too. Uniforms made children proud to learn. She was lucky, they said.

She worked for rich people. Her Madam *gave* her old clothes. Other Madams made you pay.

But mine, Selina told them, gives the best things to poor white people. And they all laughed at that. Poor white people! Hee-hee! Hee-hee!

Anyway, she is too small, Selina said. Tiny feet and tiny dresses. She pinched her fingers to the size of a fly. Poor white people must be very, very tiny. They all laughed again.

Selina, you are a city girl now, they told her. You are one of us.

Selina nodded. She counted her things. A carpet on the floor. Two mattresses already on the bed. A pink glass vase with florists' bows from the Madam's bouquets. Kotex. Mum. Two pairs of shoes. And now a wireless of her own to plug in anywhere.

The white child is growing, they said. Your Madam is too old for having more babies. You must look for another job.

Hayi! Selina said. Soon Agnes would leave to get married. No more Agnes.

Good riddance to bad rubbish, they said.

I could cook, Selina said. Who cooks on Agnes's day off? I watch her when she's not looking. I can copy recipes out of a book.

"MADAM—"

"Yes, Selina."

"When Agnes she go—"

"Yes, Selina?"

"Madam, I can cook."

"*You* want to be cook?" The Madam liked to sound surprised.

"Yes, Madam."

"There's a lot to learn."

"I can learn, Madam."

The Madam frowned, pretended to think. "All right, Selina. You've been a faithful and honest nanny. I'd like to give you a chance."

"Thank you, Madam."

"I'll tell Agnes to start teaching you tomorrow. Mind you, listen carefully."

"Yes, Madam. Thank you, Madam."

"OH LORD ALMIGHTY," Selina hummed as she stirred the soup. "You took my nephew, I gave you a cow. You took my light-skin, bad-luck sister. Don't take my light-skin child from me. Every day I sing to you and you can hear, I know. I kneel down every night. I read your Bible. Sometimes I do bad things. But I say sorry. I am human, you know that. You have punish me. My time is nothing. My sadness is nothing. I am nothing, I know that. Working, working for my child. And praising the Lord, I sing my song to you. But you know that. You know everything already."

William

WHEN WILLIAM WAS TAKEN ON AS HOUSEBOY, HE was fresh from the kraal. Jasmine, the cook, preferred them that way. They weren't so cheeky yet, she told the Madam. She herself would teach him proper English, and how to wash so he didn't stink. The Madam should leave it to her.

Leila Stone understood the art of keeping a cook. She usually allowed Jasmine some say in the choosing of a new houseboy. She knew when to complain about too much salt and when to ignore a flop. And she stayed out of the kitchen. When other women, preparing special dishes with their own hands, uncovered petty theft and nests of cockroaches, Leila thought it served them right. She said so to Maurice, sipping gin-and-it on the verandah, looking out to sea.

"They haven't a *clue* how to run a household!" she scoffed. "It's like conducting an orchestra. You can't suddenly plunge down and grab someone's violin!"

No one, not even Maurice, understood the virtue Leila had always made of her complete indifference to the domestic arts. But there were other lies that the Stones held between them, a whole life of false virtues that bound them together more than any child might have done. There was their indifference about money, for one. And, cousining that, a claim to the sort of style associated with old money. Many of their friends had made fortunes from scratch, lived in grand houses and filled them with things from overseas. Maurice and Leila loved to laugh at this, and to be complimented on their own quiet good taste. Their friends, however, laughed amongst themselves; they knew that Maurice's modest salary was signed away each month on things that didn't last. And that Leila's famous wardrobe amounted to little more than carefully chosen mark-downs from end-of-season sales.

AFTER SUPPER ONE night Leila rang the study bell for Jasmine.

"What's going on up there?" she asked, tossing her head towards the dark outside, the servants' quarters above the garage.

"It's that William," Jasmine answered. She frowned down at the slate in her hands to show she'd prefer to discuss tomorrow's menus.

"Sounds like dozens of them. What are they doing making all that racket?"

"Singing, Madam." Carefully Jasmine traced over the

words "sweet" and "corn" and then blew the chalk dust into the air.

Leila coughed. "Jasmine, *what* are they singing? And *why*?"

"Special hymn, Madam. William he like to help people. He help me with my vein."

"Your *veins*! *How?*"

"Special medicine, Madam. And the special prayer. No more paining now."

The next night Leila sent Maurice up to investigate. "It could be dagga," she said. "Or shimiyaan. Who knows?"

But when Maurice pushed open William's door and the singing stopped, there was William sitting cross-legged on a tea crate, his huge black naked belly hanging over a skirt of skins and furs. On a small table to the side were three golden syrup tins and some empty aspirin bottles. "Master?"

The crowd of dark bodies turned away slightly to hide their faces. The heat of the small room, heavy with the smell of the Primus stove, of sweat, and of samp and beans, made Maurice plunge his hands into his pockets for balance.

"It's all right, William. I just came to see what all the noise was about."

He heard himself say "noise" instead of "singing," but his English habit of downplaying things still ran strong in moments of embarrassment. Leila was better at this. She knew without thinking what words to pick for servants, what to put up with and what not to. She explained that servants' quarters depressed him because he hadn't known them as a boy. He didn't feel protected, as she did, from coming down in the world.

A baby began to fret.

"Well," said Maurice, "carry on then, William. But please keep it down. The Madam has a headache."

MOST OF WILLIAM's clients came to him from Mac Hattie's Private Zulu Hospital, just over the hill, behind the Presbyterian Church. At Mac Hattie's, modern medicine was practised for a fee. The doctors struggled with antique equipment and long queues and diseases too far gone for treatment. Their patients listened politely to how and when to take their pills, and not to stop regardless. But then, when they felt better, they saved up the pills and sold them to a friend.

"I THINK JASMINE'S in this too," Leila said at lunch.

Maurice nodded. "Quite probable," he said. "A little pocket money."

"I think she touts for him at the bus stop. All those hordes coming and going to Mac Hattie's. She's always out there on some pretext or other."

"I'm going to instruct William to keep the hall window shut," he said. "All we need is one of them waltzing down here from the bus stop with a knife. You just have to read the papers these days."

"Ah!" cried Leila. "Things are not what they were, are they?" She loved the phrase, the balance of are and were, the hint at some cause for nostalgia.

He looked out of the window, right into the eyes of a chameleon, had he seen it in the mango tree, swinging slightly on the end of a branch.

Leila brushed her cheek with her fingertips. Her skin was soft and dry to the touch, her proud flesh loosening from the bone. Lately she had been watching in fascination as the eyes of men passed over her.

"One day," he said, "you'll be a widow. I've begun to worry about it. The money part I mean."

From somewhere deep in her stomach panic rose and stuffed itself into her throat. She laid down her fork. The turgid, dimpled piece of roe on her plate sickened her. Another time they would have laughed. "Freud, thou shouldst be living at this hour!" as she took a large bite and clacked her teeth together and he winced. She would have rallied to his talk of death. But now she saw her skirts lengthened and shortened season to season. She heard her friends say, "Leila's not what she was, you know." She was choked up suddenly with the old age neither of them had considered it worth saving for.

AS IF MAURICE had given death a welcome, someone stabbed Jasmine at the bus stop that night, and ran off with her money. William burst into the study screaming, "Master! Master! Big, big trouble!"

The crowd on the pavement parted to let Maurice through. They had laid her out on the bench and shuffled back now beyond the arc of the street lamp. Jasmine was still alive. Her breath gurgled up through the blood in her lungs and mouth.

"Has someone sent for an ambulance?" Maurice shouted into the shadows.

No one answered.

"Well then, for God's sake, *run* you big baboons! Run to Mac Hattie's! RUN!"

EVERY DAY WILLIAM carried aspirin bottles of coloured water to Jasmine at Mac Hattie's. Leila rang up and spoke to Dr. Singh.

"Dr. Singh? Mrs. Stone again. How's my Jasmine today?"

"Not much improvement, I'm very sorry to have to say, Mrs. Stone. But nor is she worse, I can happily tell you. Tomorrow is another day, is it not, Mrs. Stone?"

Leila returned to the yellowed pages of Jasmine's recipe book.

"Sponge," she said. "This morning we're going to make a sponge, William."

"Sponge, Madam."

"All right. Three eggs."

"Three eggs, Madam."

"And did you get out the mixmaster?"

"Yes, Madam."

"Flour. Baking powder."

William hovered behind her.

"Well?"

"Baker powder?" he asked.

"Bak*ing* powder," Leila snapped. She stared up at the bank of kitchen cupboards.

William danced around on his bare feet, opening one cupboard after another and then standing back, like a magician, to reveal its contents.

Leila peered into a few. "Who knows?" she asked a shelf of grimy bottles filled with herbs and spices.

William shrugged and smiled sheepishly. "Unghas, Madam," he said.

The bell shrieked, number three flapped down.

"It's the Master in the study," she said. "Please go and see what he wants this time, William."

Alone in the kitchen Leila rested her forehead against the fridge. The old age that had choked her at first nested now just under her ribs, crowding her heart.

"Awu, Madam!" William whispered, back on his silent feet. "I find a baker powder, Madam. Don't be worry."

"HOW'S WILLIAM MANAGING on his own?" Maurice asked, trying to fork up a piece of dry sponge.

The question irritated Leila. So did the sponge left on Maurice's plate. It was the sort of flop Jasmine would have kept for the servants. Jasmine had always known just where to go wrong and how. Leila uncurled her finger from her teacup and brushed it across her cheek. She didn't want to learn all this, not in the time that she had left.

"William will be fine," she said. "He's quick and willing. I'm just getting him through the basics."

WHEN MAURICE BUCKLED over his coffee a few nights later, clutching at his chest, the crowding around Leila's heart began to break up. Sitting beside the stretcher in the ambulance and then in the hospital waiting room, she felt her heart billow. Three words—not even words yet, but leaps and trembles in her blood—gave a new rhythm to her breathing.

Serves him right. Serves him right. Serves him right.

FOR TWO WEEKS Maurice and Jasmine lingered in their separate hospitals. At home meals happened somehow, tins of sardines, sardines on toast, an omelette one day. William said he was watching Beauty, next door's cook. He produced a pudding made with Nestlé's condensed milk and chocolate digestives.

Leila praised him for each new thing. Then, with care, she suggested modifications.

"William, try some Tabasco in the soup next time. Little-little—" She flicked her wrist twice. "Just like that, see?"

"I'm do it, Madam," he said, nodding with the gravity of a teacher's pet.

One day he suggested shyly that she could let him do the shopping. Not just trips to the Greek's shop with a note when things ran out. Checkers would be cheaper, he told her. Save her lots of money.

"William," Leila announced at the hospital, "has the illiterate's gift of memory. Do you know that he came back from Checkers this morning with every item correct? What'd gone up, price per kilo, the lot!"

Maurice stared at an arrangement of anthuriums on the table at the foot of his bed. The flowers stuck up out of their florist's clay stiff and alien. He felt far from home and longed, after all these years, for England.

"I think we'd be amazed," Leila was saying, "how much he makes from that business of his. Twice his wages easily I would think."

"Unless I recover fully, darling, I think we'll have to sell the house," Maurice said. "We could rent something smaller, a townhouse perhaps."

"Townhouse?" She laughed. "I've never understood what they mean by 'townhouse,' have you?"

"It has an upstairs and a downstairs, and it's one of several, usually in a row."

"What about William?"

"William?"

"It would have to be near Mac Hattie's," she explained. "We can't expect him to give it all up now, can we?"

"I would have thought Jasmine more to the point," he said.

Leila dropped her voice. "She died last week, darling. They found the bugger, you know. It's murder now."

"Died?" He raised his head slightly off the pillow and turned to stare at her.

"It was a foregone conclusion. That's what Singh said anyway. There was no good time to tell you."

"Who took care of everything?" he asked politely.

"I did. I paid Mac Hattie's. Her son came for the body. Don't worry, I remembered to give him money for a goat."

"Everything's happening at once." He sank back and stared at the ceiling.

"Rubbish!" she cried, her old rally. "I'm managing beautifully!"

Every night now there was singing in William's room. They came flocking in at lunch time too, down from the bus stop, up the steps next to the garage, carrying their bottles with them. She'd given up trying to get him to weed or clean the windows in the back of the house. He liked to be in the front, within sight of the bus stop, so that he could call things out to his patients.

"The pension's going to be very little, Leila. I'm not quite old enough. Please Leila, listen to me. You can't go on running your own life if you can't pay for it."

The wind dropped out of her heart and left her limp. "Every day," she said, "someone's chauffeur delivers a cake to the house. What am I supposed to do with them? I let William take the lot."

"I'm sorry, Leila." He closed his eyes to squeeze the tears out of them.

"It serves me right," she said. "There's nothing to be sorry about."

WILLIAM WAS WAITING when she returned from Maurice's funeral.

"We pray for the Master tonight," he said.

"Thank you, William. You can go now. I won't be wanting supper."

He stood his ground, staring at the floor. "Madam can lock her door tonight. I sleep in the house."

She smiled. "Oh no, don't worry. You sleep in your room, William. Thank you very much anyway."

But when she woke the next morning she stopped in the passage outside her door and sniffed. She lifted her dressing gown and, steadying herself against the wall, dropped slowly to her knees. Then she bent her face to the carpet. He'd been there. The carpet still radiated his fresh onion sweat and the grass of his sleeping mat.

That evening Leila settled into one of the verandah chairs with a sherry to watch three ships leaving the harbour.

"William!" she called out.

"Madam."

"Tomorrow I'd like you to go through the Master's clothes and take whatever you want. Sell the rest. You can keep the money."

He cupped one hand into the other and hung his head. "Awu, Madam," he said.

"Do I smell fish tonight?" she asked. The sherry had made her hungry.

He nodded.

"What kind? Something new?"

"With mango, Madam. Beauty she show me."

"You're very clever, William. Very clever indeed."

Leila dressed for dinner. She made up her face and put on her mother-in-law's diamond clasp and earrings. "Let's have the candlesticks," she suggested. "And the blue linen placemats, William, and the napkin to match."

His fish was better than Jasmine's, firm and sweet. He had learned to do new potatoes too, and to sprinkle them with parsley.

"Par excellence!" she cried.

William peered at her soberly. This smiling and laughing made no sense.

"Coffee on the verandah tonight please, William," she said. "And, for God's sake, open the windows. It's very close indoors."

"Awu, Madam, the Master he say——"

"The Master is dead." There was a new happiness in saying things. "Things are not what they were," she chortled into William's gleaming round black face. "You can't go on living your life if you can't pay for it, can you?"

"Madam."

"Look, William, this sleeping on the floor is absurd! Make up the divan in the Master's dressing room and sleep there if you must. So what?"

She pushed back her chair and, touching familiar things as she passed them, made her way out onto the dark verandah.

Songbird

WHEN I WENT TO ANSWER THE DOOR, I ASSUMED Lena would be just another distant relative who had survived the Holocaust. There had been a number of such survivors in our house throughout my childhood—a time spent in the shadow of that magnificent evil, compared to which, as my mother often said, what could matter? And yet the visits of the survivors—except for people like Aunt Gertie, who were sufficiently prosperous or educated to seem like everyone else—were confined to the afternoons. Usually, they came alone. They toiled up the hill from the bus stop, sat through tea with very little to say, and then went away again with a bag of our old clothes. But now here was Lena, clattering into the living room and shouting, "A piano! A piano!" with the intention, clearly, of sitting down to play before the afternoon was over.

She was a sturdy woman of middle age, with a home-bleached thatch of hair, and a flat, wide, Eastern European face. Without waiting for an invitation, she flopped down at one end of the couch, flung her arms and head over the back, planted her knees apart and flapped her skirt. "Whew!" she said. "Ai! I'm shvitzing!" Thick, dark hair curled on her legs and in her armpits, and she smelled raw with sweat in the dead summer heat.

With her arms up, I could not see whether she still had her numbers. Some did, some didn't. All my mother had told me was that once Lena had been quite something, that she had survived the camps in the way young women had often had to, poor devils, they had no choice. And, as usual, my blood had quickened at the thought.

My mother rang for tea, and began to tell Lena about the school I went to, the choir I sang in. Survivors, she would explain, sometimes liked to reminisce about their own childhoods before the War. Talking about me was a convenient way to introduce the subject.

But Lena was only interested in the piano—how old it was, what make. "Once, I was quite a songbird," she offered, accepting her tea and then stirring spoonfuls of sugar into it.

"What sort of singer?" my mother asked. When survivors said "once," they generally meant "before," and it was safe to ask.

"Opera, everything. I was quite a songbird," she repeated.

"Well, I hope you'll sing for us." My mother sliced the

cake, and then handed a plate to her, another to me. I
thought, perhaps, she would ask me to play, too, and to
sing. Usually she did, and I loved to perform. But people
like Lena didn't love to listen, that I could see. In fact, she
hardly noticed me at all, hardly seemed to notice even
my mother. Lena, my mother would explain, had passed
through the valley of the shadow of death. And the
phrase, whatever it meant, would swallow me up with terror. At night, on the way down to sleep, I often hovered
on a precipice overlooking that vast, dim, chill terrain.
And I knew I could never survive it.

"As a matter of fact," said Lena, "singing saved my
life."

My mother sat forward, so did I. Seldom did the visits
of survivors produce more than hints and sighs about the
lost years, never a story. My mother heard the stories
from Aunt Gertie, who was a sociologist, and was writing
a book. They tell them to each other, she would explain to
me. Who else could comprehend the horror of it all?

I myself had chased down the horror in book after
book, stared into photographs of the barracks and the
ovens and the pits, into the faces and bodies of the barely
living and of the dead. To one book I returned again and
again. It described how young women in the camps had
been used for sex by German soldiers, how they had been
made to do knee bends every morning to prepare them
for lying in bed all day, taking on soldier after soldier.

When I asked my mother why the knee bends, she simply said that certain muscles must have needed to be stretched, poor devils, and who but the Germans could think up such debauchery?

Every night, I thought of it. Sometimes, I did a knee bend in front of my bedroom mirror, wondering whether, after all, I would have qualified for that sort of survival, and which muscles mattered for the purpose, how even Germans must have loved the women a little or how could they have done it with them? How could they have wanted to do it?

Lena swallowed her tea, and stood up, wiping the palms of her hands on her skirt. I could see the numbers now, there they were.

"No more tea?" my mother asked.

Lena shook her head and made straight for the piano, where she settled herself onto the bench, adjusted it this way and that, threw open the lid, and played a few chords.

I tried to catch my mother's eye, but she angled herself away from me, crossed her legs with a swish of stockings. I reached for the teapot and poured myself more tea, stirred loudly.

"Shhh," my mother hissed over her shoulder.

This irked me. My mother herself was the one who would wink at me when my cousin sang "Hark, hark, the lark!" after dinner on a Friday night. It was she who would entertain us, after everyone had left, with an imitation of that dreadful falsetto, and the mouth pursed up, and the mincing curtsy. But now—with Lena running arpeggios up and down the piano, all mistakes, and then landing loud and flat on her opening note—now she would not even turn around. And Lena's singing was much worse than my cousin's.

Lena sang some sort of Slavic song in a minor key, turning her face towards us like a nightclub singer. She squeezed her shoulders forward, pushed out her lips, opened her mouth wide and square, with her tongue arched strangely in the middle, very moist, and quivering. It was impossible to believe she could ever have been quite something.

I pretended to inspect my fingernails and sighed and tapped the table with my shoe. Several times, my mother turned and frowned, but I ignored her.

When she had finished, Lena actually bowed, and then strode back to the couch, trailing her ripe odour. "That is what I sang," she said. "I can never forget it."

"How could one forget," my mother murmured, "if it saved your life?"

She poured her more tea and cut another slice of cake. When survivors came, she kept tea going all afternoon, offered the cake again and again. For them, she would explain, it's as if it happened yesterday. A crust of stale bread, a bowl of watery soup—that's all they had, year in, year out.

"All my life," said Lena, "I have been lucky. Some people think that's a funny thing for me to say, but I say it anyway because it is true. Even as a child, my mother said, 'This songbird has a lucky star'. When I arrived at the camp, I was singing, right there on the platform. One of the guards came over. I thought he would clout me with his club, but he didn't. In fact, he took a liking to me. He got me a job in the kitchen."

"Ah," my mother sighed. "How long were you there?"

"In the camp? Almost two years."

I could only think of Lena and the guard in the kitchen, Lena and the guard in his room.

"But that's another story. What I'm telling you is what happened in the end, when they knew they'd had it, the Nazis. They were killing us off like mad before the Allies could come in and see what they had done. When my turn came, it was early in the morning. They put us in a truck and drove us into a forest, and made us take off our clothes and walk naked to a place where they had dug a deep pit. We knew what was coming, of course."

Suddenly she leaned forward. "Is it okay that I tell this with the girl here?"

"Oh yes," my mother said softly. "We don't believe in sheltering her from the evils of history."

But the way Lena was rushing through her story, the matter-of-fact voice she used in the telling—this did not at all match what I had read. Not even by looking closely at her face could I tell what it might have felt like to have been her.

"There were bodies already in the pit from the day before," she went on, "and four or five SS guards with their guns, smoking cigarettes, waiting around for us. My guard was there. He was the one in charge. It was my lucky star. He looked surprised when he saw me walking up to that pit. Probably he thought I was dead already. They had moved him long ago to another camp, but that's another story. Believe me, a man without memory is like a fish without eyes. I called out to him, 'Please, sir, let me have one wish. I would like to sing'."

"'Okay,' he said. So I sang that song. And I can tell you, I have never sang that way again, and I don't mean good, I mean loud. I yelled out that song so that the Lord would hear me. I was starving and I was freezing, but my voice sailed over the tops of the trees. And then, suddenly, a miracle happened. Out of the forest came American soldiers, shouting, pointing their guns at the SS. All night, they had been there, waiting for daylight. And then they heard me singing, and they came running!"

She shook her head and closed her eyes and smiled. My mother smiled, too, and sighed. Even I could not help smiling. I had expected Lena to tell us that she had rendered the Nazis powerless with her singing, that, like Orpheus, she had led the other naked women past them, out of the forest to freedom.

"What happened to the guard?" I asked.

"He? Who knows?" Lena shrugged. "I never asked, I never knew."

When she had gone, my mother said, "It's not a good idea to ask about the fate of the tormentors, darling. There are things the survivors would rather forget."

"But he saved Lena's life," I insisted.

"I suppose he did," she said with a slight sneer. "One way or another."

"What do you mean?"

She tossed her head. "Well, it wasn't her singing that saved her, I can tell you. Although if she wants to believe it, who can blame her?"

"What do you mean?" I said again, breathing lightly.

"According to Aunt Gertie, the story is that, when Lena saw that guard of hers, she cried and begged him to let her sing for him one last time. He refused. But he did take her aside somewhere, ordering the other guards to carry on with the ghastly business. And then the Americans heard the gunfire and came rushing in. Darling," she said, stroking my arm, "it was really Lena who saved Lena. She was quite something in her day, I hear."

I looked away. I could not bear the pleasure my tears would give her. Nor could I bear the thought of that guard forgotten, or of Lena changing the story around to suit herself—Lena, who had been quite something, and was nothing now, like me, who would never be quite something, would never have been quite something then either, although I was a showoff like Lena, boastful and vain like her, and what would have saved me, what would save me now from sitting one day in someone's house, offering to perform my life for strangers, twisting it and stretching it so that there was a past to speak of, maybe even a future, but no present, nothing of my real self?

The First Rule
of Happiness

THE TRIO WAS SEATED AT THE BEST TABLE IN the dining room, with a view right out over the mountains.

"Who *is* that man?" the old woman kept demanding, peering across at her daughter. "Get rid of him, won't you, darling? I don't like the look of him at all."

The daughter had secured the table for them, and a two-bedroom bungalow close to the main building of the hotel. She had also ordered a wheelchair in which to move her mother about, and interviewed one of the maids, who would stay with the old woman if she and Tom wanted to go for a hike or a ride. But her mother would have nothing to do with a wheelchair or a strange maid. And because she was in danger of falling down one of the rockeries, or up a step, or anywhere at all, the daughter had always to be beside her.

"It's Thomas, Ma," the daughter said, with a quick

smile around the dining room. "You remember Thomas? What's the matter? Don't you like the lamb?"

The old woman huffed down into her shoulders and pushed her plate away. "I want to go home," she said. "This place is not what it used to be. And I've had enough of *him.*"

Tom laughed. He was not going to let the old cow unsettle his delight at being included in this holiday. And so he was taking what he considered to be a philosophical view of the matter. Having lived the hard and oddly carefree life of someone who had always had to muddle through with little or nothing, he understood that fate can turn you around in unexpected ways. When Antonia would bring him her own small anxieties, one after the other, he would say with perfect equanimity, Naked you come into this world, my darling, and naked you will go out.

And she would always laugh. It was her mother who was going out of this world, naked or clothed, she would say, and God knows what havoc she'd manage to wreak before she did so. She said this, but he knew that she counted on him to understand that her mother's happiness ruled her life. He did understand, or, at least, he saw that mother and daughter were held together in a sort of grip of need—one to give, the other to snatch for herself. And that, until the old cow died, this was the way it would have to go on.

The girl from reception was moving around the dining room, table to table, with a clipboard. "Anyone interested in a helicopter ride tomorrow?" she was saying. "It takes about an hour and a half. Want to give it a try?"

By the time she reached their table, Tom had heard the whole patter. "Have you got a brochure?" he asked.

The old woman sat forward. "Who's that girl? What does she want with him?"

But Antonia's attention was now fixed on Tom. He wanted to go, she could see that. He was like a child when something new came along that he could add to the idea of his life. How many people can say they've taken a helicopter over these mountains? he would ask her. How many people can say they spent an hour and a half in one?

He turned the brochure over and examined the cost. "Wow," he said, handing it to Antonia.

"A-hey, and a-hey, and a-hey!" sang the old woman. "Is anyone there?"

Antonia looked at the price and shrugged. It was high, but when she thought of his easiness with money—his own, when he had it, hers when she offered it—she couldn't hold it against him. "Thomas Mahon," she said to the girl. "M-A-H-O-N."

"Just one of you?"

Tom shook his head. "I'm not going without you," he said. "Can't we get one of the maids in for an hour and a half? What can happen in an hour and a half, for Christ's sake?"

"I'm not going to sing anymore," said the old woman, lifting her nose in the air. "They stopped me!"

Antonia reached for her hand. "Who stopped you, Ma? No one's stopping you. Go on."

"I won't."

"Room number?" said the girl.

"No," said Tom, "I'm not going alone. Take my name off."

HE HAD AN Irish temper, as he'd explained it to Antonia, she'd just have to watch out once she got it going.

Well, it was in full swing now, but what was the point of watching out? He was turning the whole helicopter incident into a test of her loyalty, storming up and down the room, bellowing, "If she were a *man*, I'd know what to do with her! Can you imagine what these people must *think*? A grown woman tied to her mother's *apron strings*?"

"Why would I give a *damn* what people think?" Antonia shouted, falling into it at last because, yes, she had seen their faces, and yes, she did care, although what could she do about it? What?

"Ask anybody!" he shouted. "Ask anybody in the whole hotel about an old woman taking your man's place!"

"*My* man!" she sneered, well into it now. "*What* a man! If it weren't for my mother, we wouldn't even *be* in this hotel! We'd be down the coast in a self-catering cottage! So, don't tell *me*!"

"*Oh!* It's her *money*?" He dug his wallet out of his

back pocket and hurled it at her in one furious gesture, hitting the wall with a thud. *"Give* it to her! Take it to her yourself! Go!"

The old woman called out, and Antonia dashed for the interleading door.

"Run!" he shouted, following her right into the old woman's room. *"Stay there!"* he yelled, walking back out and slamming the door behind him, throwing the bolt for good measure.

EVERY MORNING AFTER that, they heard the helicopter lifting into the air. And then they would see it, darting and hovering along the ridge of mountains, disappearing behind the clouds.

"What's the noise?" the old woman always asked. "What happened to that man who was always hanging about?"

For some days, he had been sitting under an umbrella at the far end of the hotel verandah, drinking. He was very drunk now, keeping a steady gaze out over the mountains. They were oppressive, he thought, menacing when they were in shadow, like now. But everywhere else that he looked, he saw an insult—people staring, people saying things about him that he couldn't hear.

He darted a quick glance along the verandah for Antonia, but no one was there except the waiters laying things out for tea. She was probably down in the old cow's room. For three days she'd been sleeping in there—she'd taken her clothes, her cosmetics, everything. And now all he saw was the two of them arm in arm—mother and daughter—and him the laughingstock of the place.

He shook his head, holding tightly to the arms of the chair. He could take the bus back to town if he wanted to, of course, let the machine take Antonia's calls. When Mary-Rose had come home a few months ago and he'd switched on the machine, Antonia had phoned day and night, at three and four in the morning, too. After two days of this, she'd just arrived at the front door early one morning, and would've made a fool of herself right there if he hadn't stepped in to explain that Mary-Rose was his daughter. So who was he to talk?—he, who had never found a way to mix his own daughter with any other woman? Who was he to force Antonia to choose between him and that old cow of hers?

He pushed himself to his feet and found his way down the steps and along the path to the bungalow. It was hot at this time of day, the smell of the thatch was sickening. A self-catering cottage down the coast would have done him just fine. They could have got a crayfish sandwich whenever they felt like it, or just got into the car and gone to the café in town. When he had Antonia to himself, he could get her to relax by just putting a stool under her feet and a glass of wine in her hand. When he had her to himself, she was a different person entirely.

He went through to the bathroom and stared at himself in the mirror. Jesus, Mary, and Joseph—nose, neck, skin—there was nothing to hide behind any more. He went to the bedroom to look into that mirror. No better, no better at all. So who would want such a piece of baggage for her daughter? Would he? Would he?

He sat on the edge of the bed. Quarter to four. People were going past, going up for tea. He heard the old woman's door open, Antonia's voice coaxing her up the step. He began to unbutton his shirt. Antonia had given it to him, just brought it along one evening. She was always doing this—a new blanket, a set of dishes because his were a disgrace, she said.

He stood up again, lonely to the bottom of his disgraceful heart. He kicked off his shoes and began to undress, avoiding the mirror. He wouldn't look into one again—not until he was sober. He'd even shave with his eyes closed tight.

WHEN HE FOUND them on the verandah, the sun was beginning to set.

"He's here again," the old woman said. "That man."

He pulled out a chair and sat down. He'd bathed and changed—Antonia could smell the hotel soap, and the Paco Rabane she'd given him. He moved his chair closer to her. "Hey, darling," he said.

"Can't you tell him to go away?" said the old woman.

Antonia folded her arms and angled herself away from him. And yet already the great ache that had settled around her heart was lifting. When her friends found ways to ask her how and why this could happen, she, who had words for everything, didn't know what to say. That he made her laugh? That somehow he quieted the fretting that dogged her life? A therapist could get to the bottom of it, they seemed to suggest, and perhaps they were right. But really, she didn't care to get to the bottom of it, if indeed there was a bottom. Had their own lives turned out so brilliantly after all those years of expensive talk? Which one of them could claim to be as happy as she was right now?

"What's on for the rest of the evening?" he asked. "Want to take a ride on a helicopter tomorrow?" he whispered into her ear.

She smiled, she couldn't help it. Even the whiskey on his breath was comforting. When she told her friends that he made her laugh like this, that every time she came to his house, he made a fire, and put a record onto the stereo, and danced her around the table he had set for their supper, they nodded, trying to understand.

"Your name's down," he said. "It's all fixed. I'll stay here with your mother."

LIFTING OFF THE ground was like nothing Antonia could have imagined. As a girl, she had often flown with

her father when there was room for her in the plane—
mostly single-engine planes that could take them quickly
to the place of the emergency. He would sit up with the
pilot, and she'd sit in the back with his nurse and his
equipment. As soon as they took off, he would unfold his
penknife and cut a green apple into quarters. It kept down
the nausea, he said. And so Antonia had seen a lot of the
country this way, eating apples—hills and valleys and
towns and rivers, all stretching out far below her.

The helicopter was quite different. It was birdflight—
soaring, swooping, hovering up against a cliff. When they
dipped into a wooded gorge, she gasped and shrieked like
everyone else. Along they went, barely clearing the trees
on either side. And then, at the end, just as she thought
they would crash into the waterfall, they rose right
through the spray, coming out brilliantly into the light.

"If the clouds lift," the pilot shouted, "we can go over
the border." He was young and muscled and earnest
about his work. If Antonia were young herself, he would
be asking her things, seeing if he had a chance with her.
She smiled. It was lovely to have all that behind her. And
to have Tom to go back to again, the comfortable gap of
years and of life that, somehow, brought them closer.

She looked at her watch. Morning tea. Perhaps her
mother would refuse altogether—refuse anything that he
offered her. Or perhaps she would be rolling into her
usual complaint that the water hadn't been boiled, the tea
was never hot enough. And then he'd try out his nostrum

on her, tell her that naked she came into this world—and, oh, Antonia would love to see that!

They landed on the flat top of a mountain, and the pilot pulled out a hamper with champagne and sandwiches. The wind was strong up there, and the air was thin. She drank the champagne, and then lifted her face to the sun and closed her eyes. How lovely the morning was. She wished it could go on and on, right into the afternoon. And yet, standing there, she could hardly remember a pleasure in her life that she had not wanted to bring to an end. Until now, it was almost as if pleasure itself lay between something she had to leave behind and something she needed to go back to. At two in the morning, she would force herself awake and out of Tom's bed to drive home. Right from the beginning, she had forced herself out of men's beds like this—back to her parents, and then to her husband, and now to her aged mother.

Well her mother would just have to survive an hour and a half without her. Her friends were always suggesting this. They were always pointing out how manipulative the old woman was, as if Antonia couldn't see this for herself. But seeing and knowing had little to do with the way Antonia suffered when she saw a solitary old woman struggling against the wind, trying to cross the street. It was as if she were watching her own mother forsaken like that—as if she were watching the sorrow of life itself, the way it leaves you with no way back.

———

WHEN ANTONIA FOUND them, they were having a pre-lunch drink on the verandah. She had asked Tom not to give her mother a drink, but of course he had paid no attention. He had put her mother's sunhat flat on her head, and there she sat underneath it, folded up around her handbag, while he talked.

He was always talking, interrupting, finishing other people's sentences. It was one of the reasons Antonia didn't mix him with her friends anymore. When she tried to explain this to him, he just laughed. She could keep her friends, he said. They were bloody awful, the whole bang shoot of them.

"Hello both of you," Antonia said, sitting down.

The old woman reached quickly for her gin and turned to Tom. "*My* father was a private doctor to a Maharajah," she said. "We had a governess, and a bungalow on the beach. And, oh, the parties!"

"So what then?" said Tom, turning his back on Antonia.

If Antonia came up to him at a party while he was talking to another woman, he never introduced her, she would have to remind him. They'd had fights about this, but it was hopeless. He only accused her of being jealous, and of course he was right, even though that was hardly the point.

"Ma," she said, "are you ready for lunch?"

"No. We're talking, can't you see?"

Antonia pushed back her chair. "I'm going in, then," she said. "See you there."

PEOPLE LOOKED UP as she came into the dining room. No doubt they had been watching her mother and Tom all morning, and now here she was on her own—a new development. Someone a few tables down waved. It was a woman from the helicopter. "Still in one piece?" she called out.

Antonia smiled, looking around the dining room. In another style of dress and hair, these people might have been there forty years before. They were part of the reason she had come on this holiday in the first place. She'd wanted to show them off to Tom, to lie in bed with him, laughing at this one and that one, to play her life for him all over again. More than this, she'd wanted them just to lie there together, with the smoky smell of the thatch and the velvet mountains all around them. It was what she had loved most as a child herself—lying there like that, thinking what she would make of her life.

They were coming in now, Tom leading her mother the long way through the dining room like a bridegroom, smiling left and right.

"Hello!" the old woman said, lowering herself into her chair. "What's to eat? Nothing but rubbish, I suppose."

When Antonia didn't answer, she pushed the menu at her. "I said what's to eat?"

"If you can't be civil, I have nothing to say," said Antonia, pushing it back.

The old woman turned to Tom. "What's the matter with *her*?"

"Oh, she's just being childish. She'll get over it."

Antonia watched her mother groping for the bread basket. A drink always made her hungry.

"Here," said Tom.

But the old woman had turned to Antonia. "Who was that man yapping at me the whole morning? On and on he went, such a lot of rubbish. I could hardly get a word in edgewise."

Tom laughed. He put the bread basket down in front of her. "That was me," he said.

"An oldish man in a blue shirt," the old woman went on, "tall and scrawny and quite grey."

"I'm wearing a blue shirt," said Tom.

The old woman turned to Antonia. "Will you kindly tell this man to be quiet?"

Antonia sighed. "That's Thomas, Ma. *He* was the one talking to you."

"*Who?*"

"*Thomas.* On your left."

The old woman grasped the arms of her chair and turned slowly to stare at him. Her hair had been squashed down by the sunhat, her nose and her ears were enormous. "*Him?*"

Tom smiled at her, he smiled at Antonia, too, and at the people at the next table.

"The one I'm talking about," said the old woman, turning back, "was old and rather ugly, and he had *terrible* rubbled skin."

For a moment, everything stiffened around them— knives and forks and glasses. People's voices, already lowered to listen to what they were saying, splintered into silence.

"*Ma!*" Antonia cried.

"I suppose he thought he was being clever," the old woman said, lifting her nose around the table. "I suppose he thought he was making an impression."

Antonia reached out a hand, and Tom took it. Usually, he would have nothing to do with public displays of affection, as he put it, but now he brought her fingers to his lips and kissed them.

"Where's the waiter?" the old woman demanded. "What's the matter with this place today?"

Antonia freed her hand and waved for the waiter. She couldn't look at the sad bend of her mother's shoulders, the frightened old eyes waiting for an answer.

Ma: A Memoir

H E'D GOT AWAY. ONLY AS FAR AS THE HOSPITAL, but still she'd been left behind. Once, she would have got into her Fiat and revved and revved and gone off in a puff of blue smoke to find him, to catch him out in the arms of another woman, perhaps. Sixty years of marriage had only heated the furious war between them.

Every day, she waited impatiently for me to take her to the hospital.

"I have a bone to pick with you," she said when I arrived.

"What bone?"

"I've forgotten."

He didn't want to see her. When she came shuffling in, he pretended to be asleep.

"Say hello, Dad," I whispered.

"Hello," he said. He was very weak, a dark, gaunt, beautiful old man, not ready to die.

She settled into the armchair and sat there quite still, staring out through her milky eyes at nothing.

"See, Ma?" I said. "Dad says 'hello'."

"Well, why doesn't he *speak up*? I can hear everybody else. Why can't I hear *him*?" She reached over and placed a hand on his arm. "Come home, Harold," she said. "You know you're putting it on."

"Will *you* tell her!" he rasped at me. "Will you tell that bloody woman that I've got cancer?"

"Ma," I said, "Dad's got cancer. Don't be cruel."

"*Me* cruel! *Me* cruel! *You're* the one mentioning—that thing!" She clawed at the arms of the chair and pushed herself forward. "Here! Help me up. And then take me home, please. Right now."

I TOOK HER OUT for a drive in the Fiat the next day, up the coast to our favourite beach hotel for lunch. "This way, Marmalade," I said, shepherding her down the steps one at a time.

"This way, Strawberry Jam," said the Indian waiter. "This way, Honeybunch."

She laughed, she giggled. "Go on, order crayfish," she suggested. "Why don't you order prawns? You love prawns, don't you?"

Driving back, I described the wild horses on the sea, the people selling beadwork on the beachfront. We were both happy for a moment.

"Hey ho!" she cried. "How old are you?"

"Forty-nine."

"How old am I?"

"Eighty-seven."

"Really? How can I be that much older than you?"

"Because you're my mother, Ma."

"Ha! Ha! That's a good one!"

"BEATS COCKFIGHTING," said my father, smiling a bit when I repeated the conversation to him the next day. Every morning and evening I went alone to see him. I put on the Bruch G minor and closed his door. The pneumonia was almost gone; he could go home to die if we could arrange it.

"Dad," I said, "Do you want to go home? I can try to deal with Ma."

He pretended not to hear. A large tear rolled down his cheek as the second movement began. "I'd like some smoked salmon," he whispered.

At home, my mother sat staring at the bookshelf with a glass of Scotch in her hand. "I did love him so," she said, "and he seemed to love me. But what happened I don't know."

"Ma, he's sick. He's in the hospital."

She blew her nose furiously and wiped her eyes. "Don't you think two people could be happy again?"

"I think they could."

———————

THE NEXT DAY, when I came to fetch her, she was waiting at the front door. "Has he died?" she asked.

"No."

"Well, thank God for that. Wearing a hat?"

"No."

"Then nor shall I."

She was the one who was meant to die first. Once she had overheard him saying to a widow, just engaged to be married, "Couldn't you have waited for me?"

"That husband of mine," she said now, "he was really very good to me."

"Your husband is my father, Ma," I said.

"Rubbish!" she snapped. "He's *my* father."

THE DAY AFTER she claimed him as her father, he died. When I came to tell her, she was waiting, as usual, to be taken to the hospital. "Ready?" she said. "I've been waiting for hours."

"Ma," I said, "Dad died. He just died." I sat down.

She covered her eyes with a hand and breathed deeply. Finally she said, "It's unbearable. I cannot bear it. Don't expect me to bear it."

"I don't expect you to bear it, Ma. I can't bear it either."

She looked up as if she'd just met me at a bus stop. "It's full of emptiness, this place," she said.

AFTER THE FUNERAL, she sat in my sister's house like a refugee. The family came in one by one, veterans of the cemetery, to deliver condolences. A florist delivered an arrangement of flowers. I brought it in to show her. She had always loved flowers. In our old house, she and Pillay, the gardener, had conspired together every week on which beds to plant with what, where to deploy the bulbs and seedlings he stole from the Botanic Gardens.

"Look Ma," I said, "you got some lovely flowers."

"Really? How nice."

"Here, I'll read you the card. 'Dear Anne, We were so sad to hear of the loss of your darling Harold. We are all thinking of you with love at this time. Peggy, Alex and Andrew.'"

She stared out at nowhere. "Gentiles," she said.

A FEW DAYS LATER, I stole her away from *shiveh* and took her to the Botanic Gardens for tea. "How long have I known you?" she asked.

"A long time."

"That's what it feels like."

She began to weep. "I don't know why I'm crying," she said. She groped into her bag for a tissue and then blew her nose loudly.

"I know why."

"My father died," she said.

"Perhaps it's time to count your blessings, Ma."

She looked up sharply. "That's a lot of rubbish and you know it!"

"But it'll be lonely without Dad to fight with."

"And to love," she said. "Same thing."

"Ma, I'm worried. You're behaving magnificently, and it doesn't suit you."

She beamed. She reached out for her scone. I put it into her hand. "Now why don't I have a daughter like you?" she asked.

Luck

Perhaps she doesn't know what waiting is, but still she's waiting for what's coming to us all sooner or later, and how long can it be, people ask, without any quality left to the life?—just look at her sitting there, folding and unfolding an old hanky.

And if she knows the afternoon has all the charm of early summer in it—grass warmed and fragrant, sun on the lily pond, geraniums overflowing their pots—they think it's because she's fallen back to afternoons like this, waiting for the girls to come home from the beach, and Harold from golf, baby chickens with rice and gravy, and quinces and cream to follow.

But she's fallen much further than that, right back to the words themselves, the lovely, lovely words, and her mother in the front row in a hat, wild with pride. And Sister Annunciation calling her in to say, "You have been given two talents, Annie Moshal. Mind you use them well."

She has, Sister, she has. There are people who can turn a whole hall around with their happiness, and she was one of them. She stood in the wings, the words drumming along her breathing. She moved out with them into the light, into the noise and the clapping, waiting for the silence. Oh, she was greedy for that silence.

When I am laid in earth, may my wrongs create
No trouble in thy breast.
Remember me, but ah! forget my fate.

Everyone here knows who she is and who she was. "She gave such pleasure in her day," they say. "That it should come to this."

"Hey ho!" she sings. What do they know of pleasure? Sooner or later they'll be stealing her words for themselves, showing off with them, wearing them around their shoulders. They'll pull out all her feathers, knock the bottom out of her jug.

Some words still come smoothly to her, the ordinary ones she used to walk about with. Now tell me again, who are you? And, Are you a person who's a long time here? It's really not wise, she says, and, Don't let them get the better of you.

When there's a knock at the door, the nurse puts down her knitting and says, "Here come your daughters, Anne." "My what?" "Your daughters." "Who the devil are my daughters?"

Sometimes the daughters bring flowers and put them in a vase and the vase where she can see it.

"Hey!" she says. "Hey ho!"

Sometimes the daughters put on music, the lovely, lovely, lovely—and she turns her head and lifts her chin, waiting.

When I am laid in earth—

"I—I—I—"

"You sang that, Ma," they say. They take the hanky and hold her hands. "Do you know who I am?" one asks.

But the lucky ring is gone, green on the little finger where it always was. "Hey!" she says. "Hey!"

Her father gave her the money for that ring when she turned twenty-one. He gave her the money to go to London too, although words meant nothing to him. Every week she wrote a letter to her mother, struggling with the Yiddish. Every day she took the tube, and climbed the stairs, listening to the lovely, lovely—round and round, right up to her teacher's door.

And then, one day, she walked out into the grey, grey, and there it was—her name on the banner at last.

"I have babies," she says, "and it isn't easy, I can tell you."

Sometimes the nurse takes her out into the garden on her arm. They walk with the others along the path, and stop at the lily pond. And even if she knows it won't go on forever, afternoons like this, geraniums and lily ponds, still she's ready to go home.

"We're lucky," says the nurse, "I have you and you have me."

But when she asks, "Where's my mother?" the nurse says, "Dead."

How could that be? They were just on the tram together, she and her mother, and the priests sitting in front of them. "That Moshal girl sings like an angel," one said to the other. And her mother couldn't help it—she leaned forward and tapped him on the shoulder. *"Mein kind,"* she said, "**mein** *kind.*"

"How many babies do you have, Ma?"

"I don't have a husband," she says. "I'm quite ready to go home."

But night after night she sees him there in the front row, just waiting to snatch her words for himself. A thief.

"Who am I, Ma?"

"Someone special."

"But who?"

"Someone marvellous."

"Hello, Mrs. Pumshtock. Hello, Mrs. Marvellous."

"Hello," she says. "Would you like to bring your mother round for tea?"

"But these are *your* daughters, Anne," says the nurse.

"Yes, and the one shows off a lot."

They all laugh then, especially the showoff, always making a noise at the bottom of the table. He'd tried to steal her too, but she'd hung on tight, writing letters every day, page after page.

It was the other who was like a bride to him, all beauty and manners as he led her down the aisle. Still, he was hers, night after night, with nothing, nothing between the giving and the taking, only the lovely, lovely, lovely—

When I am laid in earth, may my wrongs create
No trouble in thy breast.

"Don't cry, Ma."

"Don't cry, Anne. Your daughters will come again tomorrow."

"But I want to *tell* her something."

"Who, Ma?" "What, Ma?"

"I—I—I want to say that she was marvellous."

"Bye, Ma."

"Bye, Mrs. Marvellous."